JOHNNY ON THE SPOT

JOHNNY ON THE SPOT

Amen Dell

COACHWHIP PUBLICATIONS
Greenville, Ohio

FOR

ANNE

WHO ALSO WANTS SATIN SHEETS, BUT
WHO WOULD NEVER ENJOY THEM IF
SHE KNEW FASCISM STILL LIVED
ANYWHERE IN THE WORLD.

Johnny on the Spot, by Amen Dell
© 2017 Coachwhip Publications
Introduction © 2017 Curtis Evans

Title published 1943
No claims made on public domain material.
Front cover: © Yoky Ikhwanto

CoachwhipBooks.com

ISBN 1-61646-410-0
ISBN-13 978-1-61646-410-3

THE CRIME NOVEL OF THE COMMUNIST

IRVING MENDELL ("AMEN DELL") AND *JOHNNY ON THE SPOT* (1943)

CURTIS EVANS

"I told you that heresies and false doctrines had become common and conversational; that everybody was used to them; that nobody really noticed them. Did you think I meant *Communism* when I said that? Well, it was just the other way. . . . Of course, Communism is a heresy; but it isn't a heresy that you people take for granted. Do you recall what you were all saying in the Common Room, about life being only a scramble, and nature demanding survival of the fittest, and how it doesn't matter whether the poor are paid justly or not? Why, *that* is the heresy you have grown accustomed to, my friends; and it's every bit as much a heresy as Communism. That's the anti-Christian morality or immorality that you take quite naturally. And that's the immorality that has made a man a murderer today."

> —Father Brown in "The Crime of the Communist"
> (1934), by G. K. Chesterton

He had made his several millions by sandbagging everybody that stood in his way. . . .

> —The Continental Op in "Crooked Souls" (1923), by
> Dashiell Hammett

Part I: Irving Mendell

For eight years Mrs. Mildred Blauvelt, a "pert brunette" detective with the New York City Police Department, Bureau of Special Services, went undercover as a Red. As part of her assignment to catch canny Communists who might have wormed their way into the Big Apple, she first joined the Ninth A. D. [Assembly District] Club of the Upper West Side of Manhattan, under the alias "Mildred Brandt." Within a year she had been cast out of the club, but, undaunted, she became affiliated with another suspect group, this one located in Brooklyn. Under her new alias, "Sylvia Vogel," she remained in the Brooklyn group until its members got wise to her game and expelled her in 1951.

Detective Blauvelt later testified several times in the 1950s before the House Un-American Activities Committee [HUAC], providing HUAC with a list of some 450 persons she had met over those eight years whom she identified as Communists. HUAC was rather interested in the Ninth A. D. Club, and Detective Blauvelt was more than willing to dish up the dirt to Frank Tavenner, the Chief Counsel to the committee. Among the 16 men and women from the club's more than 100 members whom she identified by name as Reds was one "Pete Mendell," the club chairman. Mendell, she noted, had appeared in the Communist newspaper the *Daily Worker* in June 1943 under the alias Amen Dell.

"Amen Dell" was the cutely conceived cognomen ("A Mendell") under which Irving "Pete" Mendell wrote his sole known crime novel, *Johnny on the Spot*, published by Mystery House in 1943. In his review of the novel in the *San Francisco Chronicle*, the esteemed left-liberal mystery critic Anthony Boucher praised it as "fast, amusing and strongly pro-labor—a rare and needed note in whodunits," while *Tricolor*—a wartime magazine edited by a leftist French Resistance figure, physicist and journalist Andre Labarthe—approvingly pronounced it "as pro-labor as any earlier mystery had ever been labor-baiting."[1] For its part the May 1943 issue of the *News of the Ninth*, the Ninth A. D. Club's cheeky newsletter, included a notice recommending Amen Dell's new novel "[f]or them as reads mysteries," deeming it "[a] swell mystery with a progressive slant." Among films, the newsletter also recommended, no doubt quite damningly to

HUAC, Warner Studio's pro-Stalin wartime propaganda film *Mission to Moscow*. Of their response to the latter production the newsletter editors hymned: "We . . . sat hypnotized, magnetized, and electrified for 2 solid hours." Dogged Detective Blauvelt turned over this issue of the newsletter to HUAC, where it was submitted into testimony as "Blauvelt Exhibit No. 12."

This was not the first time Irving Mendell had become an object of suspicion in a HUAC investigation. Back in 1938, the year HUAC (as it came to be known in 1946) was formed, the committee, which was chaired by conservative, headline-grabbing Texas Democratic congressman Martin Dies, had subpoenaed Hallie Flanagan, the national director of the Federal Theatre Project [FTP], an important New Deal Works Progress Administration [WPA] program. HUAC wanted Flanagan to respond personally to charges that under her administration the FTP had become infested with Communists.

The FTP had been established in 1935. National director Hallie Flanagan previously had been a theater professor at Vassar, one of the United States' most elite women's colleges. As national director of the FTP, Flanagan was tasked with reviving moribund commercial theater, creating employment opportunities and hope for thousands of stage actors, directors, writers and technicians who had been thrown out of work not only by the impact of the Depression but by the rise in popularity of the cheaper mass media entertainment alternatives of film and radio.

In 1935 Flanagan had made Irving Mendell head of FTP's personnel department and in 1937 she put him in charge of the FTP's "Living Newspaper," an innovative theatrical form designed to present factual information on current events to popular audiences. Promoting social action was a conscious goal of the Living Newspaper, with plays such as *Triple-A Plowed Under* (1936), illustrating the plight of Dust Bowl Farmers; *Injunction Granted* (1936), championing workers' unions; *Power* (1937), detailing the struggle of the public consumer to find affordable electricity; *Spirochete* (1938), dramatizing the medical fight against the scourge of syphilis; and the popular *One-Third of a Nation* (1938), adapted in 1939 as a film starring Sylvia Sidney and Leif Erickson, which addressed the crisis in urban housing.

Perturbed by the success and perceived radicalism of the FTP and other New Deal programs, conservative congressmen used HUAC to investigate what they viewed as subversive, anti-American agitprop. Under pressure from HUAC, the FTP—and with it the Living Newspaper—was defunded and disbanded in 1939. Controversial plays that were then in development, such as *Liberty Deferred*, which detailed the dark history of slavery and lynching in the United States, were never performed, much to the satisfaction of congressional conservatives, who did not want such negative aspects of American history examined, especially at taxpayer expense.

As the current supervisor of the Living Newspaper Unit, Irving Mendell was one of the "subversives" upon whom the hostile gaze of HUAC focused. In testimony before the committee, Wallace Stark, an obviously embittered former employee of the FTP, attacked Flanagan in part for having hired Mendell, whom he derided not only as a "candymaker from Brooklyn" but an "avowed Communist." Excerpts from his congressional testimony follow:

CHAIRMAN DIES: While you were there working on that project, did you know personally of any communistic activity that took place there?

MR. STARK: Yes. At the very beginning of Mrs. Flanagan's taking over the office, she put in a man by the name of Irving Mendell, a candymaker from Brooklyn.

DIES: Was he a Communist?

STARK: Yes, an avowed Communist.

DIES: An admitted Communist?

STARK: Yes.

DIES: What position did he occupy?

STARK: She [Flanagan] put him at the head of the personnel department to induct people into the Federal Theater in the different units.

DIES: Did he bring other Communists into that project?

STARK: Yes; several from the unit of dance music and drama where I taught, even the students that I taught.

DIES: What took place with reference to communistic activities after he became head of the personnel division?

STARK: He was afterward transferred to the Living Newspaper, which was supposed to be the unit that advocated the overthrow of the Government type of plays on the Federal Theatre.

DIES: Do you charge that Mrs. Flanagan participated in communistic activity?

STARK: I have seen reports on several plays and read several plays that she has produced up in Poughkeepsie [home of Vassar College].

J. PARNELL THOMAS [Republican Congressman from New Jersey]: Have you ever had any connection with Mrs. Flanagan?

STARK: No. She has avoided every opportunity I have had to offer any constructive plans of mine, of my organization, which I represented, to have a veterans' project on the Federal Theater.

DIES: What organization do you represent?

STARK: I do not represent any at this time.

DIES: At one time did you represent an organization?

STARK: I was one of the deputies of the Veterans' Association.

DIES: And then you base your statement that she engaged in communistic activity upon these plays that were produced by the Federal Theatre Project?

STARK: I do, sir.

DIES: What were the political theories of the project?

STARK: From what I understand—

DIES: Not from what you understand, but from what you know. What do you know?

STARK: The propaganda plays, the putting on of propaganda plays.

DIES: What kind of propaganda, to do what?

STARK: To advocate Communism, social-problem plays of a revolutionary nature. And I hope you can suspend Mrs. Flanagan.

DIES: That is not within the province of this committee.

In 2004 Sean Patterson, then a graduate student at the University of New Orleans, drew on this testimony for his UNO thesis: a play entitled *Get Flanagan: The Rise and Fall of the Federal Theatre Project.* In his play he imagined an informal conversation concerning Irving Mendell, Hallie Flanagan and the FTP taking place between Wallace Stark and a trio of philistine HUAC members:

STARK: I worked for the Federal Theatre, briefly, around the time it started. Do you realize Hallie Flanagan has employed known Communists in the project?

DIES: You have names?

STARK: Yes, I do. Irving Mendell. Flanagan put him in charge of placing people in different units of the project.

THOMAS: Was he a Communist?

STARK: Yes, an avowed Communist.

THOMAS: An admitted Communist?

STARK: That's what avowed means, sir. And you know what's really insulting? I'm a professional, right? A professional in Manhattan. Mendell was a candymaker. From Brooklyn.

JOE STARNES [Democratic Congressman, infamous in real life for having questioned Hallie Flanagan about whether Christopher Marlowe and a "Mr. Euripides," whose plays the FTP had staged, were Communists]: And he worked for the Communists?

STARK: He recruited students from the dance and drama unit where I taught. Then he was transferred to the "overthrow the Government" theater they do, the Living Newspapers. That's Flanagan's doing as well.

DIES: So, you're saying that Mrs. Flanagan herself is a Communist?

STARK: I wouldn't say that exactly.

DIES: Not even off the record?

STARK: Read the reports about the plays she did up at that girl college in Poughkeepsie, before she was even part of the project. That's enough for me.

THOMAS: You ever talk to her about it?

STARK: No. She avoided every opportunity to speak with me about anything constructive. I had ideas about organizing a veterans' unit . . .

THOMAS: So you don't know her personal political theories?

STARK: Look at the work, gentlemen! They put on propaganda plays. They advocate Communism. All these social-problem plays that won't quit until they start a revolution. All they do is find fault with the government and make it out to be an enemy of the people. Apologies to Ibsen.

DIES: Who's that? Is that another Communist?

STARK: Who, Ibsen? He's a playwright.

DIES: Funny name. He a Russian?

STARK: He's Norwegian. He wrote An Enemy of the People.

DIES: Never heard of it.

STARK: It's about a man who's shunned by the very community he's trying to help. The same way our American government is being shunned by the Federal Theatre.

DIES: Thank you, Mr. Stark. You're a good American.

STARK: I hope you're going to suspend Hallie Flanagan.

DIES: Uh, that's not within the province of this committee.

THOMAS AND STARNES: But we're gonna try!

Sean Patterson obviously detected condescension in Wallace Stark's identification of the upstart Irving Mendell as a mere candymaker from Brooklyn, but just who was Irving Mendell in those days? Was he, as Stark had claimed, really a Communist candymaker from Brooklyn?

Irving Mendell, future author of *Johnny on the Spot* and object of suspicion in the eyes of zealous anti-Communists, was born in New York City on May 5, 1904. The 1910 US census listed as his father and stepmother Jacob and Roxie Mendell. Jacob, who was probably born in 1866, migrated around 1890 to the United States, apparently either from Russia or Romania. (My guess is a borderland between the two countries, Bessarabia, or perhaps the major port city of Odessa.) Roxie, a college graduate, was born in New York around 1888, when Jacob was already in his early twenties. Seven of Jacob's nine children, including Irving, presumably were borne not by Roxie but by a previous wife. Irving was the youngest in this first set of children.

Originally Jacob Mendell was in business as a produce merchant, but by 1910 he had indeed become a candymaker. That year he patented the memorably named "Mendell's Jiu Jitsu Kandi Suker," the title alone of which is a mouthful. It is generally believed that in the United States the mass manufacture of hard boiled sweets on sticks had been inaugurated only a couple of years earlier by a gentleman from New Haven, Connecticut named George Smith, who dubbed his delicacies after a popular racehorse of the time, "Lolly Pop."

In any event, Jacob Mendel obviously knew a sweet thing when he tasted it. He, Roxie and an elder son, Alfred, incorporated the J. Mendell Candy Company, with capital stock of $40,000. It was located at 1251 DeKalb Street, Brooklyn, just three-tenths of a mile from the Mendell home in the neighborhood of Bushwick. (The Mendell home, originally built in 1899, still stands today, though the candy factory has been torn down and replaced by a modern senior living center).

In 1926 Jacob Mendell died in his sixtieth year and was buried in Mount Zion cemetery, a large Jewish burial ground in the borough of Queens. In 1930 the widowed Roxie still lived in the family home with her two daughters, Sylvia and Eleanor, supplementing her income by taking in a few gentleman lodgers. Son Alfred seems to have carried on in the candy business, having the same year patented an improvement in the merchandising display of "stick like articles, such as the so-called 'suckers' or 'pops.'" By 1940, however, the company appears to have gone into receivership.

One of Alfred's and Irving's sisters, Rose, was a public high school teacher, while another, Martha, became a physician at the Jewish Hospital of Brooklyn. In 2008 it was reported that Martha Mendell had vociferously protested in 1952 against the American Medical Association's exclusion of black doctors from its ranks, damning the racist policy as an "international disgrace." In the 1940s she also was a vocal advocate of national health insurance, an idea still deemed "radical" by many Americans today.

So, what of Irving Mendell himself? Contrary to Wallace Stark's dismissive reference to him as a candymaker from Brooklyn, Irving seems to have had nothing to do with the candy business, at least as an adult. (As a youngster it appears that he may have been employed as a messenger boy there.) Jacob Mendell died when Irving was 22, and three years later the young man had married a woman named Anne, originally from Chicago, and found employment as a life insurance salesman.

How Irving Mendell came to the notice of Hallie Flanagan in the mid-thirties is not clear. He seems to have become involved in theatricals, writing three plays, which, sadly, went unproduced. By 1937 he had become the managing supervisor of the FTP's Living Newspaper unit, which put him front and center in the political controversies embroiling the FTP. His eminence was short-lived, however, for two years later, in February 1939, he was dismissed from his post by George Kondolf, New York City director of the FTP. Upon firing Mendell, Kondolf declared that the ousted supervisor was "completely and utterly incompetent" and that Hallie Flanagan agreed with him in this assessment. Kondolf claimed that in the previous eighteen months Mendell had submitted to him not one "acceptable" Living Newspaper script. (This would be since *Power* and *One-Third of a Nation*.)

A Congress of Industrial Organizations [C.I.O.] union of WPA supervisors countered that Mendell's dismissal was "part of a campaign to wipe out the unions in the Federal Theatre." They pointed out that, contrary to Kondolf's claims, Mendell's work had been praised in the WPA brief prepared in answer to charges made against the FTP in testimony before HUAC. During his tenure at FTP, Mendell had been an outspoken defender of union rights.

After he left the FTP, Mendell joined the Ninth A.D. Club, of which he had become the chairman by 1943, the year Mildred Blauvelt infiltrated the group. During this period Mendell also become a father, his wife Anne having given birth in 1940 to the couple's daughter, Judith, after a decade of marriage. Until Judith's birth, Irving and Anne, who worked as a stenographer for a private welfare agency, lived in an apartment on Charles Street in Greenwich Village, the setting for *Johnny on the Spot*. Distinguished literary denizens of Charles Street for briefer periods of time include James M. Cain, Sinclair Lewis, Woody Guthrie and Hart Crane. Around the corner lived noted academic—and mystery fiction fan—Mark Van Doren. After Anne's birth the small family removed to "the fresh air of uptown New York" (quoting from the back flap of the jacket of *Johnny on the Spot*), where Mendell worked on his crime novel, a thriller about Fifth Column activities in the United States during the early years of the Second World War.

On the back flap of *Johnny on the Spot*, "Amen Dell" was unapologetic about the book's labor advocacy, avowing that in the labor movement there were "organized millions" who had "formed a bulwark against Fascism" and offered America "a promise of a fuller, more complete Democracy." The author pronounced that he had launched on writing mysteries because "they are the average man's type of reading," amplifying thus: "Stenographers, housewives, students, teachers, truckmen, mechanics, war workers, electricians, cashiers and dozens of other categories—all like mysteries. I like them—because they are America. So, I write mysteries."

In a time when so many mystery writers were concerned to show how highbrow, really, mystery writing could be and how mysteries were read by the world's elites—intellectuals, statesmen (i.e., politicians), judges and captains of industry—it is interesting to see an American mystery writer from the left taking an entirely different point of view, humbly defending crime writing on the grounds that it appeals to the everyday masses. Unfortunately, no other mystery is known to have appeared from Irving Mendell's hand, and I do not know what happened to him or his family after 1943, except that he died in March 1979, when he was 74 years old. Anthony Boucher, who had pronounced that "Amen Dell" was one of the most promising crime writing newcomers of 1943, was wondering what had become of him three years later, in 1946. "Only their draft boards know," he wrote of Amen Dell and other vanished crime writers of promise.

Part Two: Johnny on the Spot

"But, Johnny, we've got to trust somebody."
"Not I! I don't trust anybody until I know where they stand. When the F.B.I. starts investigating Martin Dies and Hamilton Fish and the rest of that crew, then I'll know I can trust them—not before."

". . . . in every country the aim is the same. . . . Make the people within each country hate each other. Put white against black, gentile against Jew, boss against worker. Keep them busy hating each other. The old divide and conquer idea."

—*Johnny on the Spot* (1943), by "Amen Dell"

Irving Mendell's crime novel *Johnny on the Spot* is a spirited war-time thriller with an engaging cast of characters, strong sense of time and place and an admirably snappy narrative pace, yet its most striking feature is the perceptible leftist tilt of the narrative. Although in their different ways authors as popular yet diverse as the Communist Dashiell Hammett and the Catholic G. K. Chesterton (both quoted at the beginning of the introduction) cast doubt in their crime writing on the morality of the capitalist system, mystery novelists from this era tended to take a far more complacent view of the western status quo, portraying political leftists as, at best, comically naïve Utopians and, at worse, dangerously unhinged firebrands. In *Johnny on the Spot*, however, Irving Mendell portrays the political state of the world in rather a different light.

In the novel, which is set during the first year of American entry into the war, the titular character is Johnny Angel, "mechanic, grade 1, at the huge Hirdler Automotive (H. A. to the public) plant," now doing defense work for the government. As his surname broadly hints, Johnny, a union representative at H. A., is on the side of the forces of light, having conceived an ingenious plan to increase war production at his factory, materially aiding the fight against fascism, though so far the higher-ups at H. A. have evinced little interest in it. In making the case that unions are essential to carrying on the war effort, *Johnny on the Spot* is reminiscent of another wartime mystery novel, *Murder at the Munition Works* (1940), by G. D. H. and Margaret Cole, prominent English public intellectuals and socialists who also dabbled in detective fiction.

Through a case of mistaken identity Johnny Angel is handed, while standing outside his third-floor apartment on Charles Street in Greenwich Village (where Mendell himself resided), a piece of paper containing what appears to be some sort of numerical code. It soon becomes clear that certain mysterious dastards are more than willing to kill to get this piece of paper back. Along with his goodhearted but luxury-loving girlfriend, Janie Allen, and a ravishing redhead suggestively named Mae Wells, Johnny soon finds himself embroiled in a murder mystery with grave implications indeed for the security of the United States.

Mendell took the opportunity in *Johnny on the Spot* not only to jab at conservative congressmen like his own personal nemesis Martin Dies and the arch-isolationist Hamilton Fish III, but also to flay crooked cops and capitalists, racists, anti-Semites and fascist fifth columnists.[2] Even Johnny's on-again, off-again girlfriend, Janie, a spirited lass evidently based partly on Mendell's own wife, Anne, is continually tempted from the path of righteousness by the lure of life's luxuries, on account of the independence they represent. "You have no idea how fed up a girl can get on R.K.O. and ice cream sodas," she sighs plaintively at one point. In a conversation with Johnny, she attempts to analyze her conflicted feelings:

> "Johnny. . . . I don't know what I'd do without you. Sometimes, I wish—well—that I could be like other girls and be satisfied with the idea of marriage and babies and all the rest of it. But I'm not and that's all there is to it. You've been swell about it, Johnny. And I promise you this: if the time ever comes when a husband and babies are more important to me than the prospect of having satin sheets and forty pairs of evening slippers and rooms full of gowns to choose from and a penthouse apartment—"
>
> She noticed his face and gripped his arm. "Oh, Johnny, can't you understand? I don't want satin sheets because they're comfortable. They're a—a token— a symbol of freedom—of independence. For as long as I can remember I've had to take orders from somebody. . . . That's why I don't want to tie myself down. To start taking orders from a husband instead of a boss. I want to be free! I'm tired of counting pennies. . . ."[3]

Johnny at one point accuses Janie of being "dumb when it comes to unions," explaining to her that he and his fellow workers at H. A. would never actually go on strike during the war: "What do you think we are, anyway? The army needs the things we make. That's what we're fighting Hirdler about. If he'd use our plan, we could turn out twice as much. But he won't listen." But where Janie may be naïve

Original cover of *Johnny on the Spot*

A Line to the
FRONT LINE

Dear Brothers and Sisters:

We know that "Johnny on the Spot" will eventually wend its way into the barracks library. We hope that all the boys find it enjoyable.

One hundred and sixty thousand IWO members say our "Gift A Month" to our boys must keep flowing. To meet the continuous increase in our Servicemen's Welfare list, we have embarked upon a campaign to raise $75,000 for the Front Line Fighters Fund, of which a substantial part will be earmarked for our brothers in uniform. The remaining amount is to be contributed to various other agencies such as China Aid, Joint Anti-Fascist Refugee Committee, Red Cross, etc.* Of course, we do not really separate all these purposes. After all, whatever helps the front line fighters against fascism anywhere, helps our own boys.

Our IWO men and women pledge their support of you in the armed service not with money alone. We are ready and geared for the decisive conflict—for the invasion of Europe. The majority of our International Workers Order members at home are doing their share to keep production going, to increase it, to keep the supply of ammunition, planes, tanks and ships flowing to you and our fighting allies.

MARCH TO FREEDOM! the Order's pageant portraying the United Nations' and our own country's historic fight against fascism, held by our New York organization at Madison Square Garden on May 23rd, was a huge success and a contribution to United Nations' unity. At this event Pvt. Cyrus Ezer, Pvt. Leonard Leader and Cpl. Sol Kittower were awarded a $25.00 War Bond each as winners of our Soldiers' Letter Contest.

We have received many of your pictures with pleasure and pride. Please continue sending us photos along with your letters.

We know that G.I. life must be a different world, what with *army-banjos*, *General's cars* and *dog-shows;* and we would be very much interested in hearing all of the details about it. So please keep writing.

Fraternally yours,
MAX BEDACHT, *Chairman*
Front Line Fighters Fund

Funds for Russian War Relief are raised independently.

Inside Flap of *Johnny on the Spot*

about unions, other individuals in the novel, like Lieutenant McWilliams of the New York City Police Department, are openly hostile. "He's just the kind of cop who goes out breaking up picket lines for his own amusement," scornfully observes Johnny of McWilliams, while policeman John Joseph Swazey opines that McWilliams would not hesitate for a minute to frame Johnny Angel for murder on account of Johnny's being a union official, because McWilliams deems unions "un-American." (Swazey himself, a decent cop at heart though something of a palooka, admits, "Before I joined the force I worked in an auto plant for a coupla years. We had a union, a good one, too. Did plenty for the men. And today it's doing plenty for the war. But that doesn't change Mac's feelings.") Similarly, as evidence of a widespread rightist conspiracy mounts around him, Johnny complains that United States Attorney General Francis Biddle "piddles over guys like Harry Bridges" (an Australian-born labor leader whom the AG tried to have deported under the 1940 Smith Act, on the grounds of his having been once "affiliated" with the Communist Party USA) while letting "rats run loose."

Mendell sees the rats, the real vermin gnawing at the vitals of American democracy, as racist rightwing authoritarians, sometimes organized in groups like the Christian Front (associated with the controversial radio priest Father Charles Coughlin), who, if not themselves necessarily Nazis, are ideological "fellow-travelers," if you will. "The anti-Labor, anti-British, anti-Russian, anti-Semitic, anti-Negro, anti-American sons of bitches!" an appalled Johnny exclaims after finally cracking the dire meaning of the coded message, rolling out in a rising wave of "anti's" all the objectionable qualities of these people. Referencing President Roosevelt's fireside chat of April 28, 1942, Johnny thinks how true it is that "Bogus Patriots and Noisy Traitors" are insidiously undermining the war effort and the country. Readers of *Johnny on the Spot* should of course rely upon their own powers of discernment to determine which characters in the novel are (and are not) to be trusted; suffice it to say here that, when you find that your neighbors read *The Brooklyn Tablet*, you might well take heed.[4]

Endnotes

[1] According to Douglas Porch in *The French Secret Services: A History of French Intelligence from the Dreyfus Affair to the Gulf War* (New York: Farrar, Straus and Giroux, 1995), the Venona project conducted by US counter-intelligence (1943-80) established that Labarthe "appears beyond doubt" to have been a "Soviet agent" (p. 134).

[2] Dies, a critic of the Congress of Industrial Organizations (a group, it will be recalled, that had supported Mendell during his fight with FTP New York City director George Kondolf), declined to run for reelection in 1944, after the CIO began a voter registration in his Texas district and found a candidate to oppose him. The same year Hamilton Fish III was defeated in his bid for reelection in his New York congressional district. Fish sourly credited his defeat to "Communistic and Red forces from New York City. . . . " Another, rather more famous, crime writer who abominated Hamilton Fish III was Rex Stout, who in 1930 built his house in Connecticut across the state border (though his mailbox was in New York), so he would not have Fish as his representative.

[3] Mendell tellingly dedicated his novel to ANNE, who also wants satin sheets, but who would never enjoy them if she knew Fascism still anywhere in the world.

[4] Spoke the President:

> This great war effort must be carried through
> to its victorious conclusion by the indomita-
> ble will and determination of the people as one
> great whole. . . . It must not be impeded by
> a few bogus patriots who use the sacred free-
> dom of the press to echo the sentiments of the

propagandists in Tokyo and Berlin. And, above all, it shall not be imperiled by the handful of noisy traitors—betrayers of America, betrayers of Christianity itself—would-be dictators who in their hearts and souls have yielded to Hitlerism and would have this Republic do likewise.

Seventeen men, all residents of Brooklyn and most Christian Front members, were arrested by federal agents in January 1940 and charged with stockpiling weapons as part of a plan to overthrow the government. Though the charges were dropped the next year, the incident assuredly was in Mendell's mind when he wrote *Johnny on the Spot. The Brooklyn Tablet* was a prominent diocesan newspaper that backed the Christian Front.

JOHNNY ON THE SPOT

All characters, situations and locations herein are fictional and any resemblance to living persons or places is purely accidental. However . . .

CHAPTER 1

Johnny Angel was tired as he climbed the stoop of his house. A quick look at his watch by the light of the street lamp showed that it was after one o'clock.

"Sleep is what I want," he thought, "and plenty of it."

He pushed open the front door, which his landlord had painted a bright Chinese red, with the misconceived notion that the color added a Bohemian touch and was therefore appropriate for a Greenwich Village remodeled job. As Johnny automatically climbed the two flights of thinly carpeted steps, he noted with annoyance that the light on his landing was out again. Have to tell the landlord about that or he'd be without one for weeks.

He had just reached down and picked his key from its safe resting place under the front door mat when a large, dim shadow detached itself from the general darkness in the hall and began to move. Angel was no coward, but the hair at the back of his neck suddenly felt very uncomfortable. It seemed to be stiff and prickly. The dim blot was advancing from the turn in the stairway.

Johnny inserted the key in the lock with a hand that quivered a little—not from fear, well, not exactly from fear. The shadow was at his elbow before he could get the door open, just as he knew it would be, and it dissolved into the figures of two men.

One leaned against the door deliberately, preventing Johnny from opening it. The other spoke in a harsh whisper.

"You Angel?" He pronounced it An-*gell*, with the emphasis on the gell.

Johnny started to say, "Yes, I'm Angel," but his throat and tongue had become unexplainably dry and what came out sounded like the rasp of a saw. He gulped and tried unsuccessfully to wet his lips with a tongue as dry as a piece of cafeteria liver.

"I ast ya somethin'. Whyn't ya answer?" came the husky whisper.

Johnny made a final effort. He had to. The menace in that whisper was too great to ignore. He felt—no he *knew*—that unless he answered immediately something would happen to him—something that wouldn't be at all pleasant.

When the words came out his voice sounded queer to his ears, but at least their meaning was distinguishable. The two men seemed satisfied with his self-identification.

"Whyn't ya say so when I ast ya?" the hoarse voice demanded. "Here, I got somethin' for ya." His hand dipped deep into his pocket.

"Now it's coming!" thought Johnny Angel, and his mind, in a panic the moment before, was all set again and directing his muscles as a good mind should. Johnny knew exactly what he was going to do in the next three seconds.

As the rasping shadow lifted his gun Johnny would give him the knee, hard, trying to incapacitate him with one kick. Then he would swing around with a prayer, hoping that he could catch the second man with his right fist before he had time to pull his gun, for no doubt they both had guns.

The man had taken his eyes off Johnny and had them on his own pocket from which Johnny expected to see a gun emerge. The man was facing him, an inch or two to his right. He couldn't have been in a better position if Johnny had placed him himself.

The hand came out of the pocket. Johnny's knee started upward—and stopped midway. The hand held something that was fluttery and unmistakably white even in the dimness.

This was no gun—it was a piece of paper.

The hand thrust the paper forward, seeking Johnny's hand in the darkness. "Here, this is for you."

Johnny watched both men go down the stairs with rubbery silence. He realized that he was shaking a little. His forehead was wet; the palms of his hands were wet. The white paper was in his right hand. He held it up to get as much light on it as he could.

"I'll be damned!" he said aloud, and his voice sounded like the croaking of a pond full of frogs. "It's a summons! And me sure that a process server was a gangster with a gat. I better stop reading myself to sleep with those detective stories."

Still feeling a little clammy, he went into his little furnished apartment.

Preparing for bed, he looked into his bathroom mirror. The figure that peered back at him was not hard to look at. It was a tall, dark, curly haired young man with slightly stooped shoulders, who had deep set, sparkling brown eyes and a not unpleasant face.

It had even been called a handsome face in certain feminine circles. But as is usually the case, Johnny had the poor judgment to be completely uninterested in the many girls who had set their caps for him; some quite openly, others more subtly, and wore his heart on his sleeve for blonde Janie Allen, the one girl who was most persistent in not responding to his charm.

A few drops of perspiration still hung on the brow of the face in the mirror. Johnny wiped them off with a flourish of his handkerchief. He looked into the deep brown eyes and spoke aloud in a voice which was beginning to return to normal. "Johnny Angel," he said. "You're as yellow as a grapefruit and you scare easier than a rabbit. I'm ashamed of you!"

Then he turned abruptly from the mirror and went into his bedroom.

Sleep was difficult. There was a let down feeling that came after the nervous tension had relaxed. As he tossed about, Johnny tried to reason the thing out. Why had he been so frightened? Why so sure the process server had a gun? Why had he felt death so imminent?

The only answer he could find was that he had been imagining things. And yet there was more to it than that. There had been such a definite menace in the way the men had remained waiting for him. And that light being out just tonight. True, it often was, but was this time a coincidence? They could so easily have turned it out.

And two men. Why should it take two men to serve a summons? And what was the summons about, anyway? He realized that in his relief he had stuffed the paper into his pocket without even looking at it.

His curiosity began to rise. His rent was paid; he owed nothing that he knew of; he had signed no notes for anyone. Who could be suing him and for what? The only way to find out, he decided, was to get out of bed and look at the summons. And while he was telling this to himself he fell asleep and had queer, uneasy dreams.

A light tapping on the door woke him, and he was surprised to find it was already light. His watch near his bed told him it was exactly seven o'clock.

The tapping was repeated.

Johnny stumbled out of bed and pulled his robe on, still half drugged with sleep. He was always like that until after he shaved and had his coffee.

He staggered through the bedroom to the little foyer and pulled the door open. Then he tried to push it closed again, but he was too slow. One of the men had his foot in the crack. Johnny leaned against the door. The men did, too. They were heavier. The door gave slowly.

The men were inside, closing the door behind them.

Johnny knew these were the same men as last night, although then he had been unable to see their faces in the dark. And this time there was no mistake about their menace, for the smaller of the men palmed an ugly blunt automatic. It was pointed at the middle button of Johnny's robe.

The small man resembled his automatic. He was blunt and ugly. There was a twist to his lips as though he were perpetually sucking on his side teeth.

The taller man was about Johnny's height, but broader and heavier. He had a saddle-back nose and peg teeth. When the big man spoke there could no longer be any doubt of his identity, for it was the same harsh whisper of last night.

"Hoist them!"

The three of them were crowded in the tiny foyer.

Johnny put his hands over his head.

Somehow, here in the daylight, even with the gun only two feet from him, he wasn't half as frightened as he had been the night before. He knew it and it made him feel good. Then it had been the concealed menace that had got him. Now, face to face with the worst, he could take it.

The big man had run his hands through the pockets of Johnny's robe. They were empty, except for a pack of cigarettes.

"Where is it?"

"Where is what?" Johnny tried to make his voice sound innocent.

"You know what!"

Johnny didn't answer.

The gun in the little man's hand began to wiggle impatiently.

"Lemme give it to him, Whisper." His voice was high and excited. "We'll find it our own selves if you lemme give it to him."

"You hold your fire, Runt," answered Whisper. "We got time for that. I want the paper first. Where is it, punk?" His heavy shoe lashed out and caught Angel on the shin.

The pain lifted Johnny higher than he had ever suspected he could jump. His upstretched hands almost touched the ceiling.

When he landed the gun was pressing into his third rib and Whisper was asking: "You gonna talk or you want some more?" His heavy shoe was raised for another kick.

"Sure I'll talk. Why didn't you say what you wanted? Is it that paper you gave me last night? All you had to do was ask for it. I don't want the damn thing. What is it, anyway? It looked like a summons. Gosh—you don't have to use a gat to get a summons back. I'd be glad to give it to you."

Johnny was talking fast and furious, and trying to think at the same time. Part of what he said was true. Sure, he'd have given the paper back and been glad to get rid of it, if, they had only asked for it. But they hadn't. They'd stuck a gun in his ribs and kicked him in the shins when he was helpless. And nobody was going to kick Johnny Angel in the shins and get away with it, gun or no gun.

"Stop the babble and pass it over."

"It's in the bedroom in the drawer of the chest."

"Which drawer?"

Whisper was already at the chest with Johnny following in a painful limp and the Runt bringing up the rear with his gun pressed against the small of Angel's back.

"Center drawer."

Whisper opened the center drawer. It was full of papers. Johnny hated to throw papers away. That drawer had electric bills up to four

years old, poems he had written during his youthful amours, elec-
tion propaganda, advertisements for radios, suits, eating places; leaf-
lets he had helped write for his union in its early days; in fact, every
imaginable kind of useless paper.

The Runt edged around to look in the drawer. Whisper ruffled
among the papers. "I don't see it here."

"I put it on the bottom, for safekeeping."

"Well, dig it out then."

Johnny's hands came down from over his head. They didn't go to
the drawer. They kept coming down. One hand, tight in a fist, caught
the Runt on his wrist, and he dropped the gun.

Whisper lunged at Angel.

Angel jumped on the bed. Two steps took him to the bathroom
door. He dove in, pulled the door shut, snapped the lock. In almost
one move he threw up the window and slithered through it onto the
fire escape.

He dashed down a flight and tried the window on the floor beneath. It was locked. The lower part of the window was opaque, the
upper part clear glass. He looked inside. There was a man standing
near the shower which was closed. His hand was inside the curtain,
as though testing the water. Johnny knocked on the window. The
man turned and looked at him. He had a peculiar look on his face. At
that moment the shower curtain was flung open. Johnny could see
a beautiful red-headed girl standing there, water still dripping from
her body and her bathing cap.

She saw Johnny. He heard her scream. The man came toward the
window threateningly.

"Classy chassis," thought Johnny, and dashed down another flight.

The window here was open. He pulled it wide and jumped into
the room. The apartment had the same layout as his own. The bathroom opened into the bedroom. It was empty. The bedroom led to
the little foyer and the hall door. At the other side of the foyer was
the door leading to the living room with its tiny kitchenette. The door
was closed. Johnny listened at the hall door.

He heard footsteps coming down the stairs. He opened the hall
door carefully, just in time to see Whisper's back going out of the red
painted front door of the house.

Johnny went out into the hall and quietly closed the apartment door after him. Then he climbed the two flights to his own floor. From the apartment below his he heard angry voices, a man's and a woman's. He grinned.

His door was open. He peeked in cautiously. Maybe the Runt and his gun were still there. The apartment was empty. The middle drawer of his chest was on the floor, the papers scattered all about the room. "I really ought to go through all that junk and get rid of it," thought Johnny.

He closed and locked his door. Then he pried open the bathroom door and went in and closed and locked the bathroom window. He looked at his watch. It was seven minutes after seven. "That's the busiest seven minutes I ever had!" he thought.

He flopped into a chair and sat quietly trying to think. In a few minutes he shook his head and said, "I'll be damned if I can figure out what's going on here."

He went over to his coat which was carelessly draped over the back of a chair, where he had thrown it the night before. He put his hand into the pocket. The paper was still there. He pulled it out and looked at it. The outside looked like a summons all right, but was devoid of all typed matter. The inside was blank except for some numbers which didn't seem to make sense. The numbers were 2668 22816312816623167196812731847684.

He sat down again and examined it from every position. It just didn't make sense.

He tucked the paper back into his pocket, grabbed off a quick shave and shower, and hustled into his clothes. He started down the steps, then thoughtfully came back and examined the light on his landing. The bulb was missing.

On the front stoop Johnny Angel ran into Mr. Ponds. Mr. Ponds owned the house and lived in the basement. He also owned, according to general rumor, a dozen other remodeled jobs in the Village.

Knowing Mr. Ponds, Johnny believed the rumor. Ponds' idea of running a house seemed to be to paint the front door red, raise the rents and let the fairies take care of the rest.

Not that the tenants didn't raise hell about the lack of sufficient heat and hot water and other such unimportant trifles. They did. But

Ponds had a way of turning the conversation into different chan-
nels when they came with their complaints. The complainers soon
realized that their only choice was to suffer or move. Most of them
moved. Then Ponds would re-rent their apartment for more money
and urbanely continue to receive complaints from the new tenants.

Johnny had long ago reconciled himself to the lack of service, for
he was not home often enough for it to be very important to him.

"Good morning, Mr. Angel. Fine day," Ponds greeted him.

"Yes, it is. By the way, Mr. Ponds, the light on my landing is gone.
I wish you'd put a new one in."

"Light gone? That's funny. I just put a new one in two days ago.
You know what I think? I think those Johnsons who moved out yesterday snitched all the good bulbs. They were funny people, those
Johnsons, always complaining about something. I'm glad they're
gone. I got their apartment rented already and for three dollars a
month more. I wish all my tenants were like you, Mr. Angel. Money
on the dot and never a complaint."

"And also, Mr. Ponds, I wish you would put a lock on this front
door. Anyone can get into the house."

"A lock? Sure thing. I'll fix it today. Like I was saying, we got a
nice lot of tenants now. I don't expect any trouble from any of them.
Quiet and respectable. That's how I like them. Quiet and respectable.
There's that girl under you. Never hear a peep out of her. You'd never
know she's there."

"Doesn't a couple live under me?"

"Couple? No. Just one girl. A very nice quiet girl. Red hair. No
complaints. And this first floor apartment—I just rented it yesterday.
Very nice quiet man. Say, first I thought he was a relative of yours—
his name is almost the same. But he spells it with two 'l's'."

"Two 'l's'?"

"Sure, two 'l's'. A-N-G-E-double L. Pronounces it An*gell* instead
of Ane-gel. You know, like Jello."

Ponds caught the blank look on Johnny's face. Johnny's face
always looked blank when he was thinking. Blank and stupid. The
deeper he thought, the more moronic he looked.

"What's the matter? Didn't you ever hear of Jello?" asked Ponds.
"You know, that Jack Benny stuff. Gee, he's hot stuff. Did you hear
the crack he made about Fred Allen Sunday night? He says—"

"Thanks, Mr. Ponds. I've got to run."

Johnny knew that if he didn't run, he'd hear the whole Jack Benny program repeated, word for word. He also knew that there would be no change in the front door status, and that if he wanted to be sure of a light on his landing, he'd better bring a bulb home with him.

But what was more important was that he knew now that the affair last night was a case of mistaken identity.

But how about this morning? Had the Runt and Whisper discovered their mistake and therefore used their gun openly? Or would the real Angell have received the same sort of treatment? And that red head! No wonder the man had such a silly look on his face when he saw Johnny at the window.

Habit had taken his footsteps across Charles Street to Seventh Avenue, then down one block to West 10th Street and across another to where West 4th Street, in its drunken, meandering way, crossed West 10th while heading north. Only in Greenwich Village could an east and west bound street take the notion to run north and get away with it. It gave the inhabitants a nice unstable Bohemian feeling and also gave them something to explain to provincials from above 14th Street.

A few doors down the street, Johnny paused before another remodeled house. It was better looking than his apartment building. The stoop had been removed and the whole front painted, instead of only the door. He went down the three steps into a vestibule. Inside was a bank of bells.

Johnny pushed the one marked Jane Allen. He gave it three short pokes and a long one. In a moment the buzzer gave him the same signal back. That meant Janie was ready and would be right down. Two long buzzes meant come up and wait.

He was a little disappointed. He had hoped she wouldn't be ready. Then, waiting upstairs, he might have had a chance to start the day right by snatching an unexpected kiss. Janie never would let him kiss her except after she'd had at least two drinks, and morning kissing was especially taboo. "Too much of a domestic flavor about it," she had said.

He went out into the sunshine and waited. He felt his mouth getting a little dry and that lump rising up in his chest. The prospect of seeing Janie always did that to him.

All she had to do was to enter a room where he was, and he'd go slightly light headed, like drinking an old fashioned on an empty stomach.

For more than two years he had been meeting her every morning this way, not to mention the evenings spent together, and still he had been unable to train that lump which rose up in his chest, to stay down in his stomach, where it seemed to stay in ordinary moments.

The front door opened and Janie danced up the three steps.

"Morning, Johnny. Swell day!" she sang, and tucked her arm in his. They began to walk.

Johnny gulped and found his voice. "Gosh, Janie, you look beautiful," he blurted.

"Oh, Johnny," her voice was plaintive, "when will you learn? I've told you a dozen times that to say a girl *looks* beautiful is only a half compliment. You imply that she really isn't beautiful, but only looks that way. Is that what you mean?"

"Stop teasing, honey. You know what I mean. You look beautiful and you are beautiful. And you're smart. And sweet. And very, very desirable. When are you going to be an angel and marry me?"

"Aha—my daily proposal! And my daily rejection. Now that the formalities are over, what do you know?"

"Plenty! I'm brimming over with excitement. But it'll hold till we get to the diner. Meanwhile, let me just think of how swell it feels to be walking arm in arm with you. It's the least you can do for the guy who's keeping company with you."

"Johnny Angel! Did you get me drunk and get me to agree to keep company with you while under the influence? Because if you did it's no fair—and I don't remember anything about it, and I won't have it!"

"Nothing like that," he interposed. "This is my own affair. You see I'm keeping *mental* company with you. You've got nothing to say about it. It's my mind and I'll do what I like with it. If it enjoys keeping company with you, it will—and don't you try to stop it."

She squeezed his hand. "Johnny, you are an angel in more ways than one. I don't know what I'd do without you. Sometimes I wish— well—that I could be like other girls and be satisfied with the idea of marriage and babies and all the rest of it. But I'm not and that's all there is to it. You've been swell about it, Johnny. And I promise you this: if the time ever comes when a husband and babies are more important to me that the prospect of having satin sheets and forty pairs of evening slippers and rooms full of gowns to choose from and a penthouse apartment—"

She noticed his face and gripped his arm. "Oh, Johnny, why can't you understand? I don't want satin sheets because they're comfortable. They're a—a token—a symbol of freedom—of independence. For as long as I can remember, I've had to take orders from somebody. Mother and Dad wanted me to be a lady. Then they—well, you know. It hasn't been easy being all alone. Always taking orders. That's why I don't want to tie myself down. To start taking orders from a husband instead of a boss. I want to be free! I'm tired of counting pennies. I want some of the luxuries of life—"

The words tumbled out in her earnest desire to try to make him see her point of view, but if they had any effect on him he failed to show it. His face was bleak as he interrupted. "Cut it, Janie. I've heard it all before. Including breakfast in bed and the French maid."

"Yes—but here's the part you haven't heard, Johnny. If I'm ever so foolish as to marry for love, you're my man!"

Johnny stopped walking in the middle of a step and almost fell on his face. He swung Janie around to him. There were little pink spots on her cheeks. "Are you admitting that—that—that—" He couldn't finish it.

"That I'm in love with Johnny Angel," she helped him out.

His mouth dropped open and his eyes were stunned. He looked as though he were preparing to have a fit.

"Johnny!" Jane's alarmed voice brought him to.

Right there on Sixth Avenue and Eighth Street he threw his arms around her and gave her a resounding kiss, to the great enjoyment of all the passersby.

"Johnny, stop!" She pulled herself free. "You're ruining my make-up."

He was panting. "Never mind the lipstick, darling. At times like this I care less than nothing about lipstick. Help me into the diner. The shock is too great to bear."

They found an empty booth in the lunch wagon and ordered their wheatcakes and coffee. Jane remade her mouth and said: "Now, you've got to understand, Johnny. I admitted I love you because I do and there's no use lying about it. But as sure as I love you, I'm just as surely not going to get married, and I don't want you to pester me about it. Do you understand that?"

"Say it again!"

"Say what again?"

"Say 'I love you' again. I've been waiting to hear that for more than two years. Say it again."

"All right. But just once." They looked deep into each other's eyes. "I love you so much," said Janie, with a softness that Johnny had never even suspected. His face took on a cherubic smile. "This," he said, "is the moment to die—when I'm at my happiest."

"And you will, at my hand, Mr. Angel, if you don't stop this drivel. We're in a public place and everyone is looking at us. Snap out of it. Talk about something else. There must be a few other important things to talk about."

Johnny just looked at her and grinned happily.

"Please," her voice was softly pleading. "I know how you feel, Johnny. I felt the same way myself when I discovered it. But we can't go around like a couple of simpering idiots just because we're in love with each other, can we? So please let's talk about something else. At least until tonight when we are alone. For instance, what happened at the plant yesterday? Did you see old Hirdler?"

Johnny woke from his happy trance. "Uh huh, we saw him. But we got nowhere, fast. I think that rat is trying to make trouble. He'd like to see the plant shut down, I bet."

"Oh, Johnny, you mustn't do that."

"Who, us? Gee, honey, you sure are dumb when it comes to unions. We wouldn't do it. What do you think we are, anyway? The army needs the things we make. That's what we're fighting Hirdler about. If he'd use our plan, we could turn out twice as much. But he won't listen."

"What are you going to do about it?"

"I'm not sure. We met until midnight last night trying to figure it out. I didn't get home until after one. Say, that's what I wanted to tell you about! I almost forgot it."

And he quickly outlined the adventures of the white paper, omitting only the part about the redheaded girl. When he finished, he took the paper out of his pocket and gave it to her. "Look—it's like a summons on the outside, but inside there's stuff typed in code. What do you make of it?"

Jane's face was a little pale. She pored over the code, then shook her head. "Doesn't make sense. Just a lot of jumbled numbers," she said. Then, "Johnny, I'm worried. I don't want anything to happen to you—now. Why don't you go to the police?"

"Maybe I will. But holy cats! Look at the time! We'll both be late."

They jumped up, leaving breakfasts which neither one had touched and dashed for the door. Johnny squeezed her hand before she ran across Sixth Avenue to get her uptown bus and she reached over and gave him a peck of a kiss on the cheek, leaving the unsuspected mark of her lipstick. "Come over to the house for supper," she called. "We'll eat in."

Johnny walked the few steps to the subway entrance and went down the steps humming.

As they had left the diner, a man rose from the booth directly behind them and followed them out. Now he dove down the stairway directly behind Johnny and was squeezed right beside him during the whole trip. But the whole Japanese army could have been squeezed in around Johnny and he would not have noticed it. Johnny Angel wasn't on a crowded Eighth Avenue express. He was riding on clouds.

CHAPTER 2

It wasn't until lunchtime that Johnny Angel, mechanic, grade 1, at the huge Hirdler Automotive (H.A. to the public) plant, snapped out of his cloud floating and got both feet back on the ground once more.

It happened when he went to his locker to get his wallet and found it gone. He searched every pocket, but there was no wallet.

He sought out his section shop steward. "Hey, Jack," he complained. "I've been robbed. My wallet's gone."

"Much in it?"

"No—just a few bucks. But it's the idea of the thing. Our clothes ought to be safe here."

"Sure, I'll check on it and see what I can find out. Positive you didn't leave it home? Did you notice it when you changed your clothes?"

Johnny threw his mind back over the morning. He tried to remember changing into his work clothes. He couldn't. The last thing he could remember was Janie pecking his cheek in very wifelike fashion. He grinned at the thought.

"Nope," he told Jack. "I can't remember a thing."

"Anything else missing? Fountain pen, pencil, watch, anything like that?"

Something smacked Johnny's brain and he jumped as though he had received a hot foot.

"Wait a minute," he said and dashed for his locker. He searched through his pockets again, this time frantically.

"Well, what do you know about that?" he demanded. "It's gone!"

"What?" Jack was puzzled.

"The paper. The summons."

"Oh. I thought it was something important."

"This was important, I think. Anyway, lend me a buck until pay day just in case I don't get my wallet back, which I have a notion I won't."

"Sure," said Jack, and passed the bill over.

Johnny sought out steel-gray Bill Lawrence over at Murray's lunch bar and as they ate told him the story of the summons, ending with the fact that the paper and his wallet had been lifted.

There were worried little wrinkles at the top of Bill's nose when the story was over. "Seems to me, Johnny," he said thoughtfully, "that you're lucky it's gone. Someone wanted that paper awfully bad."

Johnny nodded. "Just the same I hate to think I'll never get even for that kick. Look." He pulled up his pants leg and Bill saw an ugly red gash which had been treated with iodine and plaster.

"Somebody ought to pay for that," insisted Johnny Angel.

Bill looked at him quizzically. "You're a queer guy, Johnny. You're lucky not to be on a slab with a bullet in your gut, and you're yelling about a kick in the shins."

"I just don't like being pushed around," was Johnny's stubborn reply.

"Well," said Bill as they walked back to the plant, "you just watch yourself. And if this business isn't finished, let me know right away and we'll assign someone to stick close to you."

"A guard? For me? Don't make me laugh!"

"I'd rather have you alive with a guard than dead alone. You may not realize it, Johnny, but you're valuable property, as far as the union is concerned. You're one of the spark plugs. It's my job as local chairman to see that you're protected. So don't be a wise guy. Let me know what happens." Then with a friendly slap on the back, Bill was off to his department, and Johnny returned to his own.

As he passed near the office door he saw a man inside. Johnny stopped and snickered. The man had a sharp hooked nose and wore heavy glasses. He was carrying his hat in his hand. His head was bald as a nut except for a tuft of hair front and center which stood up like a *skeezik's* lock. The baldness surrounding the tuft was fiery red. "Something obscene about it," thought Johnny, as he went on to his bench.

It was almost five o'clock when Johnny heard a suave voice at his side saying, "John Angel?"

The speaker was in his early thirties. His voice, clothes and bearing bespoke Harvard. He could easily have been a model for a collar ad. He wore an expensive tie clip and a pair of cuff links which must have cost the equal of two weeks' pay for Johnny.

"Yep!" Johnny was brusque because he didn't like Harvard type men.

"I'd like to talk to you, please."

"Talk away. I can hear."

"Privately, if you don't mind."

"Sorry. I'm on working time." Then he felt a little ashamed of his rudeness and added: "But I'll be through in five minutes if you can wait."

"Glad to," the young man nodded cheerfully. "I'll see you at the gate." And without waiting for an answer he walked away.

As he cleaned up his bench, then changed his clothes, Johnny wondered why this well dressed tea sipper had been allowed into the shop. Strangers weren't welcome there.

When he left the shop gate, the young man joined him. "Where," he asked, "can we talk?"

"Between here and the subway," said Johnny. "I've got to get home. I have a date for dinner."

The stranger shook his head. "It'll take longer than that, and besides there are too many people around."

Johnny shrugged his shoulders.

"Tell you what," young Harvard proposed. "I've got my car around the corner. Suppose I give you a lift home and we can talk on the way."

The memory of Bill Lawrence's words flashed across Johnny Angel's mind. He hesitated.

"Afraid?"

Johnny threw him a look of scorn. "Nuts. Where's the car?"

He was surprised at the car. It was low slung and seemed long enough to hold a hundred-yard dash in. A chauffeur in livery was separated from the rear compartment by a glass which rose and lowered at the touch of a button.

"Where to?" asked Harvard.

Johnny gave Jane's address and the car moved effortlessly.

"Drink?" asked the young man. He pulled a handle at his elbow and a shelf with four bottles and glasses was exposed.

Johnny shook his head.

The young man poured himself a stiff Cutty Sark and tossed it down. Then he turned so that he faced Johnny. "Well, we can start," he said. "My name is J. P. Hirdler, Junior."

If he had expected his name to cause a sensation, he was disappointed.

"I was beginning to suspect that," said Johnny. "Not many guys with heaps like this have the run of the shop. What do you want?"

"Dad was telling me about your increased production plan."

"It's the Union plan, not mine."

"I know. But you started it and did most of the work."

"So old J.P. told you about it?"

"Yes."

"I don't see how he could. He wouldn't even listen to it."

"I know that. That's why I'm here. I want to help."

"Seems to me old J.P.'s got all the help he needs."

"No, you don't understand. I want to help you."

"You mean—about the plan?"

"Exactly."

"Wait—let me get this straight. You—J.P.'s son and heir, want to help the Union to get the increased production plan into the plant in spite of your father's opposition to it?"

"Right!"

Johnny thought for a few seconds. "I don't get it," he said. "Keep talking."

"Well, Dad's wrong, and I know it. That's all. He feels that he'd be losing face if he agreed after having said 'no,' so he just keeps on saying 'no'."

"And while he keeps saying 'no' we're turning out less than half of what we could," said Johnny bitterly. "And the army needing our stuff like blazes. Many a soldier that dies for lack of equipment can lay his death on J.P.'s shoulders."

J.P. Jr. nodded sadly. "It sounds harsh, but I'm afraid it's true. However, I want you to know," and there was a sharp edge to his voice, "that you and your Union haven't got a monopoly on patriotism.

I love my country just as much as you do—and for that matter, so does Dad. His anti-union attitude is a hangover from the days before the war. Things are different today. That's why I want to know about your plan. If it really will increase production, I'll get it into Dad's head even if I have to spoonfeed it to him. Now—how does your plan work?"

Johnny thought for a minute while young Hirdler waited.

"Well," said Johnny at last. "I can't see any harm in telling you. It probably won't do much good, but it can't do any harm. It's public enough. We were planning to give it to the papers if J.P. wouldn't use it—so I guess it's all right to tell you about it.

"First, there's the business of coordinating the departments. The way it works now, there is no overall plan. Take the new gun we're making. The barrel takes longest to make. No matter how many sights and locks and stocks are made, you can only have as many complete guns as there are barrels. Isn't that so?

"Naturally," agreed Hirdler.

"Well—then why is it that while men in the other departments are getting in each other's way and turning out excess parts, the department that makes barrels is short of men, and no new ones are being trained for that work? That's just one little example. But how can we expect to coordinate manpower on a national scale if the management of a single plant doesn't seem to be able to do it—or," he gave Hirdler a piercing look, "doesn't want to do it."

He continued before Hirdler could answer. "Our plan would do three things. First: allocate and train manpower so that all departments would coordinate their work. Second: simplify certain operations so that more could be turned out per man. Third: run the plant in three shifts. Put all three points into operation and the same plant with the same machinery could turn out five times as many guns as we do now."

Johnny went through the whole plan with special emphasis on rotating shifts to keep the machinery going twenty-four hours a day, seven days a week. Young Hirdler listened, asked a few pertinent questions, and made notes.

Angel talked earnestly and at great length and was annoyed to hear Jane's voice break in with a cheery, "Hello, Johnny!"

He wondered how long ago they had arrived at West 10th Street. Jane, with her arms full of packages, was looking in the open window of the car.

Johnny leaped out awkwardly and took some of the packages. J.P. Jr. stepped out after him.

"I'm sorry you've got to go, Angel. It's been very interesting. I'd like to know more."

"Another time," said Johnny. "You've enough to start on."

"If," Janie said matter-of-factly, "you boys have something to talk about, why don't you both come up? For that matter," she flashed a smile at Hirdler, "I might even invite you to stay for dinner if Johnny would stop being rude and introduce us."

Johnny, embarrassed, gave an imitation of Zazu Pitts with his hands full of packages and performed the introduction. All three went up to Janie's apartment.

Johnny was burning up. He had looked forward to being alone with Janie. It was hard for him to conceal his annoyance.

Janie, who knew exactly how he felt, busied herself very efficiently, and soon the table was set and the food on the fire.

Once inside, J.P. Jr. seemed to forget all about his interest in the production plan and spent his time looking at Janie's pictures and books, and making complimentary remarks about them.

Johnny sat morosely alone until called to dinner.

A few cocktails which Janie had mixed while the meat broiled, helped put Johnny in a better mood and the food was served just the way he liked it.

After dinner, Johnny and Hirdler washed and dried the dishes. Young Hirdler took it as a lark. Johnny was far from sparkling. He was waiting for J.P. Jr. to leave.

Everything was tidied up. Johnny was beginning to feel good. He couldn't see any reason for Hirdler staying much longer. Soon he'd have Janie in his arms.

Then he heard Janie saying, "If you haven't anything special to do tonight, Mr. Hirdler, why not stay awhile."

"Glad to," J.P. Jr. answered. "If you'll stop being so formal and call me Hirdy. All my friends do."

"O.K., Hirdy. And that Miss Allen business is out, too. I'm Janie."
Johnny's groan was audible.

Janie smiled. "I do believe he disapproves. Not that it'll do him any good. He knows I'm interested in how the other half lives. Tell me, Hirdy, what sort of sheets do they use at your house?"

"Why—er—uh. I don't know just what you mean."

"I mean are they linen or satin?"

"Linen—I think."

"Don't you know?"

"I never paid particular attention."

"Look," she led him to her bed. "These are linen. Hearn's best. Are yours like that?"

"Yes—I think they are."

She pouted in disappointment.

Johnny said: "I told you that movie was the bunk."

"Nonsense," she replied. "Just because the Hirdlers don't use satin sheets is no sign they can't be bought. And if they can't be bought, I can have them made, can't I?"

Young Hirdler was looking at both of them, puzzled.

Johnny put his forefinger to his head and revolved it as though showing wheels in motion. "Nuts!" he explained solemnly. "From her mother's side of the family. The old lady was scared by a Ku Kluxer in a satin sheet. Janie was born that way. Then she saw them used in some silly movie. Now it's her idea of luxury and she won't be happy until she has them."

"Seems like a very sensible idea," said Hirdy. "I'll ask Mother as soon as I see her."

"There! That's an attitude I like." Janie resumed her catechism. "Now tell me, do you train your own servants or do you get them that way? Movie butlers are always so perfect."

Johnny showed his disgust with a snort. It seemed to him that the talk went on forever. He went to the closet and took out a bottle of rum and poured himself a stiff drink. After his fourth, Janie, who hadn't seemed to be noticing what he was doing, called out: "Better lay off, Johnny. If you take another you'll have a hangover. You always do."

Johnny defiantly gulped the fifth. He felt better. "Maybe," he thought, "it's because of the rum. But at least she knows I'm here."

He went over and joined the conversation. Hirdler was explaining how his sister shopped for her clothes.

Johnny barged in with: "That reminds me, Janie. You know that code? It was lifted. Had my pocket picked, or something."

Hirdler stopped talking.

Janie looked surprised. "Why, you couldn't have, Johnny. I have it."

Johnny stared.

Janie laughed. "You look just like a fish. Here, I'll show you." She got her bag and pulled the summons out. "We separated in such a hurry this morning," she explained, "that I forgot to give it back to you. When I got on the subway I found it in my hand. So—I put it in my bag and here it is."

Johnny took it and put it in his inside pocket.

Hirdler was looking at his watch. "It's almost eleven," he announced. "Time for me to go."

"Oh, but there's so much more I want to know," Janie cried.

"I'll come again if I may."

"Do. Just give me a call when you can make it."

When they were alone, Johnny sat looking at Janie. His head felt very light. He got up and poured himself another drink to stabilize it. He looked at her some more. Finally he said, "I'm sore."

She said calmly, "I knew you'd be."

"Then why'd you do it?"

"You know why."

"Yeah—I know. Those satin sheets. I bet you'd sell your soul for satin sheets."

"You shouldn't drink if it makes you think things like that."

"Well, anyway, you'd marry a man who could support you in satin-sheet style." His tongue got a little twisted on the last three words.

"Yes," Janie was thoughtful. "I think I would. But that's not the same thing."

"No," he became scornful, "that wouldn't be selling yourself. That would be respectable!"

"You have no right to—"

He cut her off. "I have! I have all the right in the world. I love you, and you love me and you should marry me and let the sheets come when they may."

"No—I won't! I warned you Johnny. This is what I was afraid of. Now you keep away from me, Johnny Angel. Keep your hands off me." She backed away from his approach, but how far can you back in a Greenwich Village apartment when twelve steps is its overall size? His arms were around her, his lips seeking hers.

"You're just taking advantage of me because I admitted I love you. Don't, Johnny. You mustn't!"

He found her lips and there was not a sound in the apartment for a matter of minutes.

Then Janie sighed. "Oh, Johnny, you're so sweet."

Johnny didn't bother answering. He picked her up, wondering why she felt so light and carried her across the room.

She said, "No," over and over, and kicked a little with her long, well-shaped legs, but Johnny didn't even notice.

Her eyes were closed and he kissed each one of them. Her cheeks were unnaturally red. Her arms were around him. She wasn't fighting any more. She was holding him closely.

"Johnny," she whispered. "Are you sure you love me?"

He nodded.

"It's not just—?" She opened her eyes and examined his face searchingly.

"No."

"You'll always love me? And respect me? No matter what happens?"

"No matter what."

She closed her eyes again and sighed.

Johnny thought frantically, "My God—what do I do now?"

It was a purely rhetorical question. But just at that moment the doorbell rang harshly—insistently.

They were both on their feet by the time it stopped.

"Damn!" said Johnny.

Janie's face was still flushed. She said nothing.

The bell sounded again.

"Ignore it," whispered Johnny. "It's probably a mistake."

They waited. It rang again, longer than before.

"I'd better see who it is," said Jane.

She walked to the door, pushed the buzzer, and pulled her door open. Johnny remained in the inner room. He heard her voice. In a minute she came back. The flush was gone. A worried look replaced it. "There's something funny about this, Johnny. It was a man who said he had a telegram for Adams. My name is plain enough on the door bell. I thought he was going to try to come in, until he saw your coat and hat. Then he went away."

"Funny I didn't hear him," said Johnny.

"He spoke in a whisper. Oh, my goodness—do you suppose it could be—"

"Was his nose sort of dented in at the bridge?"

"Yes! Enough to ride it bareback. And his teeth were funny, too!"

"It was Whisper all right."

"But how did he know you were here?"

Johnny shrugged. "Maybe he followed me. I don't know. But now I've got two scores to settle with him, and the kick in the shins is the lesser of the two."

He snapped off the light and went to the window. Outside he could just barely see a man lolling against a stoop rail across the street. "He's waiting for me," he muttered.

Janie grabbed him. "Johnny, I'm worried? Let's call the police."

He shook her off. "No, I'd have to give them the summons. I'm going to find out what this is all about before I bow out of it. Get your typewriter."

She pulled her portable Royal out of the closet. Johnny gave her the summons. "Make a copy of this."

"But why—?"

"So that if they get the original, we'll still have an 'in.' Go ahead."

She made the copy on a blank sheet of paper. "Now where can we hide this?" asked Johnny. "They may come looking for it."

"I know a good place," said Janie after a moment's thought. She folded the paper, then took a chair into the bathroom. Upon the wall was a fuse box with a snap cover. She opened it, put the folded paper inside, and snapped it shut.

"Good," said Johnny. "Now I've got to get home without them nabbing me."

"Johnny, I'm frightened."

"Don't be. You'll be all right."

"Not for me, you dope. I'm frightened for you."

"I'll be all right, too."

"Phone me as soon as you get home."

"All right."

"If I don't hear from you in fifteen minutes, I'm going to call the police."

"Make it a half hour. And so long as we have a copy of the paper, I'll bring the original around to the police station in the morning. Good night, darling." She gave him her lips without any hesitation.

Instead of going down, he went up to the roof. Jane's building was one of three of equal height. He tried the roof door on each of the others. Both were locked.

"Looks like the fire escape again," he said.

He picked the one on the corner house. That would let him out on the side street. He went down slowly and quietly, and reached the last flight without having aroused anyone. There was a detachable ladder for the last flight down. Johnny decided against using it. Too much noise.

He stepped over the iron rail, lowered himself a little and then dropped.

He landed on something hard and squirming that gave way beneath his weight with a loud grunt. It was hard, yet there was a certain unmistakable softness to it.

Johnny bent down and turned it over. It was the Runt. Johnny wasn't even surprised. It seemed right that the Runt should be where Whisper was. The Runt was out cold. Johnny had hit him squarely, and if the knocking of his head on the stone walk hadn't been enough to put him away, Johnny's 180 pounds landing hard on his kidneys would have been.

Johnny peeked around the corner. Whisper was still leaning against the rail across the street.

Next to the house was an old garage remodeled into what the owner called a charming one-family house. It was set back from the building line.

Johnny picked up the Runt and sat him down in the shadows of the garage. A gun fell out of his pocket. Johnny picked it up and looked at it speculatively. He put it into his own pocket.

He sauntered down the street. When he got to the corner he quickened his pace. He was almost running when he reached his own house.

The hideous red door was a very welcome sight. He was glad there was still no lock on it. He pushed it open and went inside.

The door to the first floor apartment was open. A noise that sounded like a person falling came through the door.

Johnny hesitated, then poked his head inside. It was dark. His exploring fingers found the light switch and threw it on.

The living room door was open. Johnny went in. A man's body was on the floor. The legs were folded up. They had stiffened in a sitting position. The body had apparently just fallen from the chair which stood next to it.

The back of the head was blown away and the coat was a bloody mess. Johnny recognized him immediately as the strange man he had seen at the plant. The hawk nose still wore the thick glasses, but the tuft of hair did not seem so obscene now that the bald head had been drained of its fiery redness. The right hand, fingers outspread, seemed to balance the figure.

Where the left hand should have been was only a bloody stump. Johnny Angel felt the rum in his stomach doing tricks.

He dashed upstairs to his own apartment and just reached the bathroom in time. When he finished in the bathroom he went into his bedroom and dialed Jane's number.

Her voice expressed her relief. "I just looked outside, she told him. "He's still there. Probably thinks you're staying for the night," she giggled.

"Hey—that's an idea. Why didn't I think of it before I left?"

"Two years of good training," she answered tartly. Then, "Listen, darling. Don't call for me in the morning. I'll ring your bell. Let's play safe until this thing is settled."

"All right by me," he answered. "I'll be waiting for you."

"Good-bye, Johnny."

"No—not yet. Say it first."

"What?"

"You know!"

"Oh, Johnny!"

"Come on. Just once."

"All right. I love you, Johnny. Good night." There was a click.

Johnny sighed. He thought of calling the police from his own phone and decided against it. Phone calls could be traced. He didn't want to be mixed up in any killing.

He went downstairs and crossed the street to the drugstore telephone.

He told the police about the dead man. When they asked who was calling he hung up.

As he went up his stoop again he saw the voluptuous red-head directly in front of him. She was just pushing through the red door. He followed.

She took her time going up the steps, wiggling her hips a little. There was a heavy, musky perfume about her.

When she reached her floor she turned so that he had to wait. She looked him over from head to toe. Then she passed her judgment. "Not so bad," she said.

"You're not so bad yourself, from what I remember."

"Umm," she made a funny little noise in her throat. It sounded like a cat purring. "What were you doing at my window?"

"Trying to get in. There was a man after me with a gun."

Her eyebrows went up. "Why? Was his wife in your apartment?"

"No. Nothing like that. Was that your husband with you?"

"I have no husband. That was a cousin of mine," she answered calmly, as though that settled that.

Johnny said, "Oh? Cousins are nice."

"Very handy," she agreed.

"Was he angry?"

"Just for a little while. He thought he'd been caught in the badger game. He got over it."

"I'm glad I didn't cause any trouble. Well, I've got to get on up to bed," Johnny said and tried to pass her.

She stood her ground, her body close to his. The perfume odor was very strong. She looked up into his face. "Next time," she said, "don't use the window. Knock on the door. I'm always glad to see my neighbors."

"Unless a cousin is visiting," Johnny amended.

She nodded. "Unless a cousin is visiting," she agreed.

She moved to let him pass.

Johnny dashed up the stairs, mumbling, "Get thee behind me."

When he reached the top he heard her call. She was looking up the bannister wall. "I like neighborly visits," she called softly. "My name's Mae. What's yours?"

"Johnny. Good night, Mae," and Johnny hopped into his own apartment as though the devil were after him.

While he was undressing he heard a police squad car siren as it pulled up in front of the house. He went into the living room and looked down on the white top of the car. Two policemen were getting out.

"Snow White and the two dopes have arrived and have the situation well in hand," he thought. He went back and climbed into his bed. In ten minutes he was asleep.

CHAPTER 3

Johnny was shaving when he heard Janie's signal ring. He buzzed back twice, hoping she'd understand and come up.

She did. "What have you put on the door knob, Johnny?" she cried as she came in. "I've got my hand all dirty." She held it out—soot stained.

"No talk until I get a proper greeting," said Johnny.

She stood on tiptoe and kissed him. "Lucky I'm almost as tall as you," she said. "It makes kissing much less effort. The way you stand there and let me do all the work is shameful. The least you could do would be to cooperate by bending down a little."

He bent down and gave her a good one. When he looked up he was staring into a ruddy face which was surmounted by an iron derby. The face grew directly out of a long coat, without benefit of neck. The coat seemed to be covering a huge, distended watermelon. The whole get-up spelled flatfoot. Johnny straightened. "What do *you* want?" he demanded.

"Hello, Romeo," said the cop. "Get your coat. The boss wants to see you downstairs."

"What about?"

The detective shrugged his shoulders and disdained to answer.

Janie was frightened. "What's it all about, Johnny?"

"I don't know. But you better get on to work. I'll tell you all about it tonight."

"The boss'll want to talk to her, too," said the detective phlegmatically.

He proceeded them down the stairs and at the first landing stood aside and pointed to the apartment door.

Inside they found Mr. Ponds, talking as usual, the red-headed Mae, looking pale and frightened, and the Andersons, who lived on the floor above Johnny.

There was a chalk outline on the floor, with a dark brown stain at one end. Johnny concealed a shudder as he saw it.

At the other side of the room stood a man in civilian clothes. He looked like a prosperous business man. He addressed the detective. "Any more?"

"No," the officer answered. "That's all the tenants. She," he pointed to Jane, "don't live here. She was in his room," a nod toward Johnny. "I figgered you'd want her in, too."

"Right. You can close the door. I'm Lieutenant MacWilliams. I want to ask you people some questions. I want to know where each of you was last night between five and seven."

They all began talking at once.

"Hold on," said MacWilliams. "One at a time. You," he pointed to the landlord.

"I was over at my other house on Jane Street," Mr. Ponds answered. "Something was wrong with the water pipes and I had to fix it. You'd be taking a hot shower and all of a sudden the water would turn cold. The tenants complained. They been complaining about it for months. I tried to get a plumber to fix it, but the rates they charge! So I went over and fixed it myself. There ought to be a law against those plumbers. They charge—"

"What time did you go?"

"About three o'clock. I remember it was three o'clock because the kids were just coming out of school. Say, those kids are a menace. You cops ought to be able to do something about them. They play ball in the street and break windows. Last month I had to put in two new panes on account of them. Why can't you keep them . . ."

MacWilliams was beginning to lose patience. "How long did you stay there?" he demanded.

"Where?" Ponds' face was blank.

"At your Jane Street house." MacWilliams' voice was hard and clipped.

"A bad man to get angry," whispered Janie. Johnny nodded.

"Oh, there," Ponds remembered. "Well, you see I had it all fixed when I found out that the pipe I had connected to the main line was a gas pipe and not a water pipe. I couldn't leave it that way, could I? No, indeed. So I . . ."

"What time did you get home?" barked MacWilliams.

"About eight o'clock. I came in together with Mr. and Mrs. Anderson. They just come back from dinner. They eat at the Perry Lane . . ."

"Never mind the Andersons!" It was almost a shout. "I want to know about you and nobody else. And from now on you just answer yes or no. When you were working over at Jane Street was anybody with you? What I mean is, can you prove you didn't come back here between five and seven?"

"Oh, sure. My brother-in-law Jack was with me. He's not working now and he used to be a plumber's helper, so I said to him, 'Jack,' I said—"

"Never mind what you said." He dismissed Ponds, still talking, with a gesture. "You, Mr. Anderson. Where were you between five and seven?"

"He came in with me," said Ponds.

MacWilliams walked over and stuck his chin into the landlord's face. "You," he said, punctuating his words with a stiff forefinger, "hold your tongue. Another word out of you and I'm going to have you gagged."

"If that works, I'll use it on Ponds in the future," Johnny whispered to Jane. They were standing together over in a corner.

"Does he always talk so much?" she asked.

"Yep! But it's not his fault. You see, he has false teeth." They kept their voices down.

"What's that got to do with it?"

"Well, his dentist is one of those experimenting guys. He made Ponds a set of plates that are attached to each other on a coil spring. You wind it up in the morning before you put them in. Ponds figures that as long as the teeth are wound up he may as well keep talking. No extra effort, you see."

Janie's small sharp heel came down on his toe and he let out a yelp.

Jane smiled angelically as MacWilliams shouted: "You two over there! What's going on?"

"Nothing at all," she said sweetly. "Mr. Angel just stubbed his toe."

Johnny made a fist at her and she wrinkled her little upturned nose at him, and they turned their attention to the questioning of the Andersons.

Mr. Anderson was letting off steam. It hissed for about five minutes before MacWilliams interrupted with, "Am I to understand, Mr. Anderson, that you refuse to cooperate with the police in the investigation of a murder committed in this very house?"

"A murder?"

There was a shriek from Mrs. Anderson as she slumped to the floor.

Jane went to the bathroom and brought a glass of water. In a few minutes they had Mrs. Anderson sitting up in a chair.

"I'm sorry, lieutenant," said Anderson. "I didn't know. That changes everything. Ask us anything you want—anything. We'll be glad to answer, won't we, dear?" He patted his wife's pudgy hand.

"Oh, Lucius," she fluttered. "I think I'm going to faint again!"

"You'll do nothing of the kind," said MacWilliams very definitely. "You'll save your fainting until I'm through with my questions."

"Yes, officer, sir!" she replied meekly. Mrs. Anderson was a great respecter of constituted authority and would never think of disobeying an officer of the law.

The questioning went on. The Andersons, it seemed, had met at the Perry Lane restaurant at six o'clock. They didn't like eating in. Dirty dishes, you know. He had come direct from work, she from shopping. He hadn't been home all day. She had been out since lunch. No, neither of them had ever met or seen the man who lived in this apartment. They knew the Johnsons who had lived there previously, but the new tenant was a stranger to them.

"It's just too awful," Mrs. Anderson whimpered.

"Not at all," said MacWilliams. "It'll give you something to tell your friends about."

"It will at that, won't it?" Mrs. Anderson brightened a little.

MacWilliams directed his attention to a new victim. This time it was the red-head. All eyes turned to look at her. She wore a tight sweater which revealed some fine points.

Jane's look was antagonistic; Johnny's full of admiration. She poked him. "Stop drooling," she said coldly. "We're in public."

MacWilliams had begun his questioning. "Name?"

"Mae Wells."

"You look awfully familiar to me. Got a record?"

"I don't know what you mean!"

"Oh, innocent, huh? You live here alone?"

"Yes."

"Where were you yesterday between five and seven?"

"At home."

"Aha," MacWilliams was all attention. "I thought we'd find that everyone was out. Now, think carefully, did you hear anything?"

She shook her head from side to side.

"Nothing that sounded like a shot?"

"No, but that doesn't mean anything. When I first moved here I used to be awakened a dozen times a night by shots. Then I found out it was the backfiring from the trucks going up Seventh Avenue. Now I don't pay any attention to them anymore."

MacWilliams said, "One person in the house and she doesn't pay any attention to shots! Did you know the man who lived here?" he demanded.

"No."

"Ever see him?"

"No."

"Did you see or hear anyone enter the house between five and seven?"

"No."

"That's all. So far, from all the help I've been able to get from you people, this murder might just as well have been committed in the Sahara Desert. But this is going to be different. You!" and his finger lashed out at Johnny Angel.

Johnny felt a queer tingling travel up his spine. "Yes?"

"I think I'll talk to you two alone. Go on, the rest of you. Be where I can reach you if I want you."

The detective opened the door and all but Johnny and Jane filed out. As Mae Wells passed, she whispered, "Good luck, honey."

Jane's ears picked up. "Who's your friend?" she demanded in a hostile whisper.

"Oh," Johnny's collar was feeling uncomfortable again. "I just met her last night on the way in."

"And she calls you 'honey' on such short acquaintance?" Jane's voice was caustic.

"It's nothing at all, Janie, honest it isn't."

Mr. Anderson had helped his wife through the door and the officer had closed it behind them. "Now," said MacWilliams, "I'm going to find out things. Sit down, you two."

Johnny sat down. Jane deliberately took a chair across the room to be as far from him as possible.

"Now, tell me. What are you two to each other."

"We're going to be married," said Johnny flatly.

"Nothing of the kind!" Janie flared. "He can marry his honey, but he'll never marry me. I have other plans."

Johnny muttered something that she couldn't hear, but MacWilliams picked it up. "What's this hurdy-gurdy you're talking about?" he demanded.

Jane flushed.

"Nothing at all," said Johnny airily. "A hurdy-gurdy is a thing that plays sweet music. About satin sheets."

"At least," snapped Jane, "it doesn't wear tight sweaters."

"Sweaters are an art," Johnny retorted. "You get out of a sweater just what you put into it."

"Some humor!"

"It's still true."

MacWilliams had been turning his head from one to the other. He looked as though he were going to explode. With a great effort he controlled himself, and when he spoke his voice was saccharine sweet. "I'm sure," he said, "that you two can hold your love-making, if that's what this gibberish is, until you answer a few little questions?"

They both stared at him sullenly, taking their anger at each other out on him.

"What I want to know is," and here the explosion could be held in no longer and the rest of the sentence came out half a shout, half a demented shriek. "What do you know about this murder?"

"Such a temper!" said Jane, shocked. "You'll never have a detective story written about you. In the books the inspector is always calm. He never gets excited."

"This isn't a book. It's a murder. Now out with it, young fellow. Where do you fit into it?"

"I don't." Johnny was still sullen.

"Oh, you don't. Well, where were you last night between five and seven?"

"I left work at five and went right to her house for supper. I stayed there until eleven."

"You didn't stop off here on the way?"

"No."

"You'll have a hard time proving that."

"Oh, yeah? Well, it just happens that it'll be very easy. J. P. Hirdler, Jr., picked me up at the plant in his car and drove me right to Jane's. He was with us all evening. He can prove my story, I'm sorry to say."

MacWilliams seemed taken aback. "You'll check on that, Clancy," he told the detective who had been taking notes.

He walked back and forth a few times with his hands behind him. He stopped in front of Jane.

She didn't even notice him. She was fuming inwardly at the deceitfulness of Johnny.

"He arrived at your house with Hirdler?" MacWilliams asked.

"What?" The question was repeated. "Yes, he did," she replied.

"And he stayed on after dinner?"

"I'm sorry to say he did."

Johnny said, "Please Janie, try to understand." But she turned away from him and looked at MacWilliams.

"Now, just what were you doing in his apartment this morning?"

"We used to have breakfast together down at the Diner at Sixth Avenue and Eighth Street." The emphasis on the "used to" cut a little slice out of Johnny's heart. "He'd call for me or I'd call him if I got out first."

"I see. Pretty close friends, hey?"

"We were." Again the emphasis on the past tense.

"We still are," Johnny cut in. "We're going to be married."

Jane gave a hard little laugh.

"I tell you I never—" Johnny began protesting.

"Enough of that," said MacWilliams. "The point is that you were living together. Isn't that so?"

Johnny jumped up angrily and grabbed MacWilliams' arm. "You can't talk about her that way."

"I talk however I want," snarled MacWilliams. "And you'll sit still and like it. Sit down." He gave Johnny a push, catching him off balance. Johnny landed in his chair heavily. He began to get up again, fuming, but Clancy, the detective, was approaching with a business-like look on his face.

Johnny stayed put. "This," he told himself, "finishes it. I might have told them the whole story of the paper, but now let the big shot find out for himself."

MacWilliams was talking. "Whether you lived together or not isn't too important. I'm not interested in your morals. The point is you were close enough to lie for each other, weren't you?"

"There's nothing to lie about," said Jane.

"Oh, no? Well, then maybe you can give me a straight answer to this one?" He had been walking again and stopped in front of Johnny. The question snapped out like a whip. "What are your fingerprints doing inside this apartment?"

Johnny gulped. "That's silly," he said. "You haven't even taken my fingerprints."

"And what do you think we've been doing from eleven o'clock last night? You're a defense worker, aren't you? Your prints are on file. We checked the records with the prints on your door knob. They match!"

"So that's why I got my fingers all sooty," said Jane.

"Yes, that's why. And we found those same prints on this door knob—both outside and inside—and all over the bathroom. Even outside the window. Now let me hear you explain that away—though I warn you it would be best for you to confess and make a plea of self-defense."

"Wouldn't that be nice for Mrs. MacWilliams' little boy? I can just see the headlines. 'MacWilliams promoted. Solves baffling murder single-handed.' No thanks, I'm not having any of that stuff."

"I'm not thinking of promotion," said MacWilliams. "I'm doing my job. That job is to find a murderer and I think I've found him!"

"You're not looking for a murderer. You're looking for a conviction. You'd arrest anyone, guilty or innocent, if you could convict him."

"If he were convicted he'd be guilty in the eyes of the law. But I'm not here to argue with you. I take it you don't intend to confess?"

"You take it right."

"And you refuse to explain how your fingerprints got in this room?"

"I never refused. I'd have been glad to answer, but you threw me off the track with that talk of confessing."

"Well, let's get back on the track. How'd they get here?"

"All right. It was—let's see—gosh, it was only yesterday morning, but it seems like years—two men knocked on my door and stuck me up with a gun. I got away by the fire escape. The bathroom window of this apartment was open. I came in that way."

"And the two men?" MacWilliams' tone showed disbelief.

"They scrammed out when I got away. When I opened this door they were leaving the house."

"And you did nothing about it?"

"What was there to do? I thought of notifying the police, but after all, they hadn't taken anything. I figured they were scared away and I was through with them."

"But you weren't," Janie put in. "One of them was waiting for him outside my house last night. He even came up to the apartment looking for him."

MacWilliams' interest in the two men was aroused. "Did you notice what they looked like?"

"Sure. I can give you a complete description. Better than that. I can even give you their names!" And he did.

"What," demanded MacWilliams, "did they really want? Stick-up men don't tail a man like that. They must want something you have. What is it?"

No bully like MacWilliams was going to get any information out of him or Jane if he could help it. Janie started to speak, but Johnny threw her a warning glance. Jane closed her mouth before a sound came out.

"I have no idea," said Johnny.

MacWilliams shook his head doubtfully. "Those descriptions don't fit anyone I know," he said. "Neither do the names. But that doesn't mean anything. They might have been imported from Haguestown or Miami. I'll see if we can round them up. Meanwhile, a few more questions. Had you ever seen the dead man before?"

"Yes," Johnny answered. "Peculiarly enough, I did. He was out at my plant yesterday at noon time waiting to see someone in the front office."

"Ever see him before that? Coming in or leaving the house?"

"No."

"Then how," and Johnny knew from the triumph in MacWilliams' voice that something was up, "did you know the man at the plant was the murdered man?"

"Why—I—"

"Go ahead, think of a good one for that. You see a man at your plant. You had never seen him before. Yet you know that the man who was murdered was the same man. There's only one answer to that, my boy. You *did* see him after you left the plant last night. Didn't you?"

"Not until after—"

"After what?"

"Nothing."

"All right. Let's try something else. Did you call anybody after you got home last night."

"Yes."

"Who?"

Johnny pointed to Jane.

"Is that true?" The question was addressed to Jane. She nodded. "What did he call about?"

"To tell me he was home, and to say good-night."

"I see. Now tell me, Angel, with a phone at your own bedside, why did you go to the drugstore across the street to make a phone call at 11:33?"

"I—I—I—"

"Oh, yes, you did. The drug clerk knows you. He noticed the time, too, because it was closing time and he had to wait for you to finish your call before he could close."

"I—uh—I really called Jane from the drugstore before I got home. I knew she was waiting for my call, so I didn't wait until I arrived home."

"But you told her you were at home already?"

"Yes."

"You lied to her?"

"Yes."

"Quite accomplished at it," said Jane.

"Or are you lying to me now?" Johnny said nothing. "Don't you think it's a little peculiar, Angel," MacWilliams went on ruthlessly, "that the phone call that reported the murder was made at 11:33, the exact moment when you were making your call from the drugstore?"

Johnny thought, "Like them or not, you've got to admit these cops get around." Aloud he said: "Quite a coincidence, isn't it?"

MacWilliams shook his head sadly. "Look, Angel," he said calmly. "Why do you have to do things the hard way? Maybe you're in the clear as far as the time is concerned. I don't know. We'll find out about that. But one thing is sure. You're in this up to your neck, and you're holding out on me. That's not going to make it any easier on you. Why don't you come clean?"

Johnny sat stubbornly silent.

Jane said: "You ought to be rounding up Whisper and the Runt. I'll bet they could tell plenty."

Johnny cast her a grateful glance, but she tilted up her nose and pretended she didn't see it.

"Then I've got no choice," said MacWilliams. "I'll have to take you with me."

"You mean you're arresting me for murder?"

"For the time being we'll just hold you as a material witness. Come on."

"But you can't do that," said Jane. "He was at my house."

"Sorry, Miss. You can go now, but we'll have to take him along."

Johnny cleared his throat and said: "Will you—uh—call Isherman and tell him?" he asked Jane.

"Yes, I will."

"Thanks."

"Don't thank me. I'd do it for a dog. Would you like some company in jail? A well-filled sweater, for instance?"

He threw up his hands in despair. Then he turned to MacWilliams and said: "Let's go."

Mr. Ponds and the Andersons were in the hall when they left and stared after them with big eyes. MacWilliams went first, with Johnny between him and the big fat Clancy. Jane followed along behind.

A car was waiting downstairs. It looked like any private car. Clancy opened the door. Johnny got in. MacWilliams followed. Johnny noticed that though the car looked like any other sedan from the outside, the inside was quite different. There were racks which held two machine guns, and other equipment, whose use he didn't understand, was packed on the floor.

As Clancy was getting behind the wheel, Johnny looked out of the window absently. He stiffened. Watching the proceedings from across the street was Whisper. "There he is," shouted Johnny, and twisting the far door open, he was out in the street.

Whisper saw him coming and took to his heels.

Both MacWilliams and Clancy sat as though paralyzed for a few seconds. Then Clancy had his gun out and was pointing it at Johnny's flying form.

If Jane hadn't awakened to what was happening there would have been no more Johnny for her to be angry at. She rushed at Clancy, grabbing his arm. "Don't shoot, you fool," she yelled. "That was Whisper he was chasing!"

"Start the car," shouted MacWilliams. "See if you can catch up with them."

Whisper had headed for Seventh Avenue and turned north. He had amazing speed for a man his size.

Johnny was no slouch himself. As they crossed Greenwich Avenue, Johnny was no more than ten feet behind. In front of St. Vincent's he was close enough for a running tackle. He dived and felt his arms close around Whisper's driving legs. Whisper went down with Johnny right behind him. Whisper lashed out with his heel. It caught Johnny square in the face, drawing blood from his nose and mouth.

Several onlookers displayed some curiosity. That is, they stopped walking and watched the chase. For the most part they watched without stopping. Some of them went so far as to cluck sympathetically and shudder at the blow Johnny received.

Johnny recoiled from the shock of the kick. When his head cleared Whisper was dashing for the subway entrance at Twelfth Street. Johnny was after him. As he reached the bottom of the steps, he saw Whisper go through the turnstile and head for a train that was waiting with its doors open.

Johnny felt for his change—pulled it out fumblingly—there was no nickel! He swore. You can't get through a turnstile without a nickel unless you jump over it. The idea of jumping over just never occurred to Johnny. The long ingrained New York habit of having a nickel handy or waiting for change at the booth was not one which could be broken at a moment's notice.

John Angel stood helplessly and watched the train bearing Whisper pull out of the station. Then he shrugged his shoulders and trudged up the steps to the street. He went up the nearest stairway—a different one than that by which he had come down.

He used his handkerchief to get some of the blood off his face. His lip was beginning to swell. His nose felt as big as an elephant's.

"I'd better," he thought, "go home and clean up a little—and find MacWilliams. He must be wondering what happened to me."

MacWilliams was doing more than wondering.

When Clancy had swung the car into Seventh Avenue, he had found himself in a mess of traffic, stopped by a red light. He pulled the siren and stuck out his head, shouting to the cars ahead, "Go ahead—let me through."

"Oh, yeah?" answered the driver of a flivver two cars beyond. "And pay a ten dollar fine for passing a red light? Not me," and he pulled his head back into his car like a turtle.

Clancy fumed and began to get out, but just then the light changed and the flivver was off like a rabbit. By the time Clancy hit Eleventh Street all that was visible of Angel was the back of him going down the subway stairs at Twelfth.

Clancy and MacWilliams reached the platform as Johnny was climbing the opposite steps.

"He made that train that just pulled out," MacWilliams decided.

"Maybe," said Clancy hopefully, "we can catch it at Thirty-fourth Street, or Times Square."

MacWilliams was scornful. "Fine chance," he snorted. "But I don't see what else we can do, so we may as well try. Open up your siren wide and let's travel."

So while Johnny was walking home, Clancy and MacWilliams were giving Old Chelsea good proof of the fact that an automobile can be a dangerous weapon. Several persons missed death by virtue of quick jumping that morning.

Johnny had expected that MacWilliams might be waiting for him in front of his house. But the front of his house was bare. He went upstairs. Mae Wells was standing by her door.

She took one look at him and said: "My God, what happened to your face?"

"Had an accident," said Johnny shortly, and tried to pass by her.

"I'll say," she made no effort to let him pass. "You come right inside and let me fix you up."

"That's all I need," said Johnny. "To be found in your apartment!"

"I get it," said Mae. "That long drink of water, Miss peachy-cheeks, wouldn't like it, huh?"

"Look, Mae," Johnny was almost pleading. "You're a nice kid. You're swell. But I got enough troubles without adding you right now. So let me go upstairs and fix myself up a little, will you, huh?"

"O.K., honey. You're the boss. But that face really needs treatment. So I'm going up with you. Oh, don't worry. I'll leave as soon as it's fixed."

In his apartment she made him lie down on the bed, with two pillows propping up his head.

She brought a basin of warm water and a towel and expertly cleaned the raw nose and lip, and painted the sore spots with iodine. Johnny winced as it burned on the open cuts. Then she got a clean towel and wrapped in it some ice cubes from the refrigerator. The cold towel was placed gently over the swelling area.

"There! That'll keep out any infection and help to hold down the swelling," she said matter-of-factly.

"Thanks," said Johnny. "You really are swell."

The words sounded funny coming through a swollen lip and a towel. He noticed a suspicious sparkle about her eyes. "What's the matter? You look as though you're ready to cry. Did I say something wrong?"

"No. No. I'm just mad. But not at you."

"What're you mad about?"

"At dames like your girlfriend. They burn me up. They get all the best guys. But when their man gets himself busted up and needs their help, where are they? Holding their noses up in the air because they don't like their man's neighbors. Oh, I know her type all right."

"Don't talk that way about Janie," Johnny protested. "She's really wonderful. She just doesn't understand. You see, she thinks there was something between you and me."

"And what if there was? It would just show that she wasn't doing her job."

"Well-ll, that's one way of looking at it."

"Here, you're talking too much. Give that lip a rest. I'll put some ice cubes out here for you so that you can keep the towel cold, then I'll go down."

She went out to the kitchenette to get the ice.

Johnny closed his eyes. The throbbing pain seemed more intense. He heard her footsteps coming back and opened his eyes.

Janie was standing at his bedside. "Oh, darling"— she had taken in his puffed face at a glance. "What happened? I chased after you, but I lost you. I thought you might have come back here— Oh!"

Mae was standing in the doorway with the pan of ice cubes.

"Oh—so your casual acquaintance is living with you now," said Janie and raged out of the apartment.

"Janie!"

Johnny tried to get up to chase after her, but Mae pushed him back. "Forget it," she said calmly. "She'll be back. It's just a touch of jealousy!"

Johnny groaned. He felt completely miserable.

"She wouldn't be jealous if she didn't love you, would she?"

That seemed to make sense.

"No, I guess not." Johnny felt a little better at the thought.

"Then stop worrying. It's good to keep dames like that a little uncertain. If she was sure of you, she'd treat you like dirt. Now, you can treat her like dirt."

"But I don't want to treat her like dirt."

"Sure not. And you needn't unless she makes you. But at least you know you can if you have to."

This very valuable feminine knowledge was making Johnny's head swim a little. A man in love doesn't think of love as a scientific game with rules of conduct to be followed if he is to attain his desire.

It is only when he is out of love that he can lend his mind to such cold thinking.

Mae said: "Keep the bandage cold. I'm leaving now."

"Thanks," said Johnny. "Make sure to lock the door after you."

Alone, he wondered what had become of MacWilliams. "I'd better try to get in touch with him," he thought. He picked up his phone and dialed police headquarters.

When the voice answered he said he wanted to get in touch with MacWilliams of Homicide. The voice told him to wait, and connected him with Homicide.

He asked for MacWilliams. MacWilliams was out, he was told. "How can I reach him?"

"If it's important we can get a message to him by radio."

"Well, maybe you better do that. This is John Angel. MacWilliams and I got separated. Will you tell him that I'm waiting for him at my apartment on Charles Street? I think it'll be important to him."

"O.K. Angel. We'll put it on the radio."

Johnny put back the phone and tried not to think of how much his face hurt. He tried to piece together the various happenings of the last two days. Somehow his mind kept shifting to Jane.

Each time he found it there he pulled it away, but each time it slowly drifted Jane-ward again.

"All roads seem to lead to Janie," he said. "I've got to square myself with her before I can do any serious thinking."

There was a loud pounding at his door.

"Open up in there!" It was Clancy's voice.

Johnny got out of bed and opened the door.

MacWilliams stormed in. There was a baleful gleam in his eye. "I'll get you for this, Angel," he said.

"What are you talking about?" demanded Johnny. "I'm not trying to get away. I even called up to let you know where I was."

"You did, indeed. And won't that look fine to my chief. My prisoner calling up headquarters to tell me where he is while I'm busting through the crowds at Times Square looking for him. I'll be the laughing stock of the bureau!"

Johnny grinned, despite his lip. "I hadn't thought of that," he said, "but now that you bring it up, it is kind of funny, isn't it?"

"Not to me, it isn't," glared MacWilliams. "Come on—put on your coat and get moving."

He picked up Johnny's coat and threw it toward the bed, then almost before it had left his hands he dived after it, recovered it and slid his hand into the pocket.

"Well, isn't this nice," he chortled as he lifted out the Runt's automatic which Johnny had forgotten completely. "I thought I felt something in that pocket. Got a license for this toy?"

"It's not mine," said Johnny.

"Of course not," agreed MacWilliams. "How silly of me to think it was." He examined the weapon. "A .32. Same calibre used on your neighbor downstairs." His voice hardened. "Come on, I've got you where I want you now."

CHAPTER 4

When they arrived downtown Sam Isherman was waiting. Isherman was a tall, slender, strong featured man—a man who knew how to grow bald with dignity. His young lively piercing eyes belied his almost hairless head.

Isherman was what is commonly termed a labor lawyer—that breed of barristers who either from a strong sense of justice or an inner need to fight for the underdog, had thrown their lot in with labor, often turning their backs on lucrative practices to do so.

The lawyer spoke to someone, and he and Angel were allowed to sit down and talk privately in a little room. "Now take it easy, Johnny. Start from the beginning and tell me everything."

While Angel talked Isherman's mind seemed to be taking the facts and setting them in little tight fitting pigeon holes. Every once in a while he would stop Angel with some pertinent question, then nod as though the answer just fit into a mental diagram.

When Johnny was finished, Sam said: "Well, it's bad enough, but not as bad as it might be. I'll make them check your alibi immediately, and if Hirdler backs it up you're in the clear. The only bad part of it is the gun. You did have possession of it, you know. But even if it proves to be the one that killed Angell, they'll have to let you off."

"How do you figure that? I should think it would implicate me even more."

"Apparently MacWilliams thinks so, too. But it doesn't. You couldn't have killed him if you were with Jane and Hirdler at the time, no matter how many guns you had. What it really does is to put

Runt and Whisper on the spot. The cops should thank you for a lead like this."

Johnny shook his head dubiously. "I hope you can make MacWilliams see it that way."

"Don't worry, I will. Meanwhile there are a few things I would like to find out."

"For instance?"

"For instance—what was the murdered man doing over at the H.A. plant the day he was killed? Why was his left hand cut off? And most important, what does that code message say? By the way, where is it?"

"Here." Johnny took it out of his pocket and gave it to the lawyer. "And when we get the answers to those questions, we'll probably be able to break this case.

"You're right. You sit tight. I'm going to talk to the law. You should be out in a few hours. I'll come up to your house this evening and we can talk this over."

"O.K. But do me a favor, will you, Sam? Call Bill Lawrence at the plant and tell him why I'm not on the job. He'll be worried."

"Sure thing."

They went out together. Isherman remained to talk to someone at a desk. Johnny Angel was led away by a policeman in uniform. He was led down some stony corridors and finally deposited in a cell. The door clanged behind him.

This was the first time Johnny had been on the wrong side of the bars. He didn't like the feeling. The clang of that metal door seemed as sharp as the slice of a knife which was cutting life away from him.

"Well," he thought, "it's only for a few hours. Unless Sam was kidding to make me feel good! But what if they do pin that murder on me?"

His knees felt weak at the thought. He turned to find something to sit on—a bed, a cot—whatever it is that you sit your life away on in prisons.

There were no beds. At the other side of the cell there were a couple of chairs. He tottered across and sat down heavily.

He took out his watch and looked at it. Eleven-thirty A.M. A sliver of sunlight came through the barred window, high on the wall.

Johnny watched the dust dancing through the sunbeams. He tried not to think, but his mind was fully active.

"Prisons!" he thought. "When you're outside you don't realize that men are in them. Men behind bars." His heart filled with sympathy for all prisoners, himself especially. Johnny Angel was feeling very sorry for himself.

He stood up on a chair and was able to see through the window. Traffic was moving at its normal pace. People were walking—talking to each other. Johnny felt very resentful. He wanted to cry out. "Hey, you, down there. Look up here. They've got me locked away, up here. How can you go on with life as usual?"

Of course, he didn't shout. He sat down again instead. "This," he decided, "is worse than dying. The hard part about dying is the feeling that everything is going to go on without you. But at least when you die you don't know what's happening. In here it goes on right in front of your eyes and you're out of it all. I might just as well be dead as far as Janie is concerned. How can I ever marry her if I'm kept in jail?"

Then with a strong will he pulled himself together and read himself a lecture. "Johnny Angel," he said, "I'm ashamed of you again. You're always making me ashamed of you. Supposing you did have to stay in jail awhile—what of it? Others have done it. Look at Tom Mooney. But that's not the point. Sam said you'd be out in a few hours. That means any minute now. You've been here two or three hours already. So why get depressed? Now buck up and be a man."

He straightened his shoulders and felt much better. He pulled out his watch to see how much time had passed. It said eleven forty-five. Only fifteen minutes! Impossible! He put it to his ear, heard it ticking smoothly.

His shoulders sagged. He knew definitely he could never be happy in a prison where time moved so slowly.

It didn't seem like a day more than twenty years when he was finally ushered out of the cell. True the few hours had stretched themselves out to six or seven, but to Johnny it seemed that he understood the most intimate thoughts and heart pangs of lifers.

MacWilliams was waiting for him.

"Well," he said, "your shyster got you out, but it won't be for long, if I can help it."

Johnny immediately forgot his distaste for jails and answered, "Go ahead—try—see what it'll get you."

"Still a wise guy, huh? All right. But I'm not finished with you yet. Remember that. And before you go. I understand you got a code message from those two friends of yours. Pass it over."

He held his hand out.

"I lost it," said Johnny. "Why didn't you ask me for it this morning?"

"Because I didn't know you had it then. So you lost it? I think I better take a look for myself."

Deftly his hand slid into Johnny's outside pocket and came up empty. When he attempted to try the inside pocket, Johnny pulled away.

"No, you don't," he said sharply. "You've got no right to search me. If I've been released, then I'm free and you'll have to get a warrant first. A man's pockets are his castle."

MacWilliams was seething. Johnny smiled. He had taken a shot in the dark. He had no idea whether MacWilliams had the right to search him or not, and anyway Sam Isherman had the code, so it didn't make a great deal of difference. But Johnny didn't like being pushed around and he felt that that's just what MacWilliams was doing.

"All right, smart guy," MacWilliams said. "I'll get me a warrant. Meanwhile, you get out of here, fast."

"With pleasure." And a moment later Angel was out on the street. It was already beginning to get dark.

He felt ravenous. The food they had offered him in mid-afternoon he had been unable to eat. He walked rapidly for three or four blocks to get away from the sight and smell of the prison.

Then he went into a cafeteria and filled himself up on typical restaurant beef stew that tasted better than anything he had ever tasted before.

He took the subway to Eighth Street and felt a kindly feeling toward all his fellow passengers.

"Everyone," he thought, "should spend a day behind bars. Then they'd know how fine it is to be free."

At twenty-five minutes after five Janie finished typing her last letter. She flipped it into its envelope, put away her notebook, cleaned the top of her desk by putting everything loose into the top drawer and locked it.

She took her bag and started for the ladies' room. She hadn't gone more than three steps when her buzzer buzzed three times. Come with your book, that meant.

She dug out her book and pencil and went into Mr. Riggs' room. Mr. Riggs of Briggs, Riggs, Waterhouse and Stevenson.

Mr. Riggs looked at her with watery, inquiring eyes. For three years he had been looking at her with those same watery, inquiring eyes, as though trying to remember who she was and what she was doing there in his sanctum.

"You rang for me." She hoped her voice didn't show the annoyance she felt. But why must this old walrus always decide to dictate at quitting time?

"Ah—yes. Miss uh Allen. Take a letter to Mr. uh Himmelweiss. Dear Mr. uh Himmelweis—no make that uh my dear Mr. uh Himmelweiss," and Mr. Riggs went on for a full fifteen minutes dictating a half page letter. He liked to think of his letters as works of art and to hurry while dictating one would have been sacrilegious.

When he finished the letter, he said: "Will you, uh, get that right out please, Miss uh Allen. And uh, I understand you were quite late this morning—uh quite late. Not a habit to be encouraged Miss uh Allen. No indeed. I certainly hope, uh, I will not have to mention it again."

Before she could answer he had turned his attention elsewhere.

She typed the letter in such anger that she made three mistakes and had to re-do it. She took the letter into Riggs' office and found his desk empty. IIis hat and coat were gone. Mr. Riggs had gone for the day!

"Oh, how I would love to tell him off. And I will, too, some day!" Janie vowed.

She left at five to six, just in time to get caught in the heaviest part of the rush hour.

At home she scrambled herself some eggs amid a deep discontent and gulped them down without appetite or pleasure. Everything was hateful—her job—her Johnny—herself.

Then, very unreasonably, she threw herself down on her bed and wept a little. The tears seemed to release her anger. In a few minutes she was feeling a little better. Still angry, still jealous, but under control.

"If," she told herself, "he thinks I'm just going to sit on the sidelines and wait for him to clear up this murder, he's crazy. And the least he could do would be to phone, so that I could hang up on him. Unless they kept him in jail."

She found herself hoping that there was that good excuse for Johnny not calling, but then the prospect of Johnny staying in jail hit her hard and she repented. She had grown accustomed to Johnny and already felt the void. Besides, she was in love with him, even if he didn't deserve it, the philandering beast.

After a few minutes of thought she had made up her mind. She tucked her silly little hat on the back of her head and left. She took the route she had often traveled before. It led to the red door on Charles Street.

She rang no bells, but went right to the apartment where the murder had been committed. She tried the knob. It opened. There was a man sitting with his chair tilted back against the wall. He wore plain clothes, but he was obviously a policeman.

"Hello," he said.

Her lips were dry. Her plans had not called for any policeman. She managed to get out a fairly normal "Hello," but was at a complete loss as to what came next.

The policeman saved her. "Sob sister?" he asked.

"Yes," she nodded violently. Why hadn't she thought of it herself? Lord knows she had read of this ruse often enough. Apparently the cop was well up on detective fiction. He seemed to expect her. "What paper?" he asked.

"The *Journal*," she answered, grasping at the first name that came to mind.

"Phooey," said the cop. "What a stinking sheet."

"Yes, isn't it? But it's a living."

Jane was back in form, and full of self-confidence, especially as she saw that the cop was giving her an admiring once over. "Some men," she thought, "still like boyish forms."

The cop got out of his chair and came over to her.

"What angles you looking for?" he asked.

"I don't know. I thought you might be able to help me. Did the murdered man have a mother or wife and babies? That would just suit for a tear jerker."

The cop shook his head.

"As far as I know they ain't been able to find out a thing about him. All they know is the name he gave."

"But he must have had some friends. Strangers don't shoot each other."

The cop struggled with that for a moment, then gave it up. "Oh, we'll find out about him in time. But so far, no dice."

"That's going to make it hard for me to write my story."

"I dunno. You ought to be able to rustle something up. If it comes to the worst, you can always write about me. I was picked as the Adonis of the staff last year. Look—a seven-inch chest expansion."

He blew up his chest until Jane was sure the vest buttons would pop.

"Oh, I'll put you in the story, all right," she told him. Why not make him feel good?

"Swell! John Joseph Swazey. That's me. Working on this case under MacWilliams. Six foot two—two hundred and five pounds. Single. I eat the breakfast of champions every morning, with fresh fruit and cream. I got a birthmark on my right thigh and I use only the tops of my pajamas. Thirty-one years old and single. I like movies with Abbot and Costello, a good glass of dark beer, and blondes—especially the tall, slim kind—like you."

He had to pause for breath and Jane nimbly cut in.

"Wait a minute. I'm not doing a Winchell. You come into this story as the strong silent detective—who does his work so efficiently and quietly that no one even notices him. But without him, law and order would go by the boards. Get it, John Joseph?"

"Yeah. But you could at least put in that I won the heavyweight boxing championship of the force in '40."

"Maybe I will. Meanwhile, don't you think I might find something to write about Mr. Angell if I sort of looked the place over?"

"You can try, but it won't do you no good. MacWilliams and I went through it with a fine tooth comb, and we couldn't find anything."

She went through the living room first. There weren't many places to look. There were a few books on the table. She leafed through them. Nothing there.

Swazey kept right behind her. "You know," he was saying, "you remind me of my old girl, Edna."

"That's nice. Thanks for the compliment."

"Yeah, she was some hot stuff. Looked kind of stand offish, just like you, but underneath it all she had a warm heart."

Jane left the living room and went to the bedroom. She looked into the closet. There were several suits hanging up. She went through all the pockets methodically.

John Joseph Swazey was right behind her.

"She had the same color hair as you, too. Boy, how that dame could kiss." He was becoming wistful. "I bet you could, too, if you wanted to, couldn't you?"

Janie wasn't even listening. Nothing in the pockets, she proceeded to the bureau drawers.

"Yes, of course," she answered absently.

"I knew it," said Swazey triumphantly. "You never can tell about these dames that look cold. That's what I always say. How's chances of you and me getting together sometime, babe?"

His chatter was just words to Jane. So long as she could keep him chattering by agreeing with him, everything would be all right.

"Yes, of course," she repeated. Nothing exciting in any of the drawers. She straightened up.

"Gosh, babe, that's swell. When?"

"When what?" she looked at him blankly.

"When are we going to step out together?" He put his arm around her waist familiarly.

"Please, Mr. Swazey!"

He chuckled. "Beats all how your type can put on a hard-to-get act. Edna was the same way."

His arm tightened, pulling her toward him. Her hand lashed out, catching him across the cheek with a resounding smack.

"Detective John Joseph Swazey," said Janie, "I shall write in my story that you attempted to attack me, unless you begin behaving yourself immediately."

The cop's arm dropped to his side and he looked at her in puzzled wonder for a moment. Then he smiled. "I get it," he said. "You don't mix business with pleasure, eh? Just like Edna."

Jane marched into the bathroom. Swazey was following. She said, "Pardon me," and slammed the door in his face.

"Phew," she whistled. "So detectives are human, too."

Her eyes flitted around the bathroom. Clothes hamper, empty. Medicine chest—toothbrush and powder, shaving cream, razor, brush, a guaranteed hair grower, bayrum—nothing more.

She noticed her face in the medicine chest mirror, and then took her compact out of her bag. On the glass shelf was a box of paper tissues. She took one out, to remove her lipstick. She reached for a second. The second tissue wasn't tissue. It was firm bond paper.

She pulled it out. It was a summons of the same type Johnny had received. She felt again. There were two more in the box. She took them out quickly and stuffed all three in her bag.

From outside came Swazey's voice. It had lost its friendly tone. It sounded like a cop's voice now. "Hey—what are you doing in there?"

Jane said, "Please, Officer Swazey!" in a very indignant tone.

He grumbled something and was silent.

She quickly applied her lipstick.

Before opening the door, she flushed the toilet. "Just to make John Joseph happy."

Outside he was waiting for her. She gave him a big smile. He began to melt immediately. Before he could ask any embarrassing questions, she said, "What time do you get through?"

"I'm relieved at midnight."

"I'll be looking for you," she said coyly.

"No kidding?"

"No kidding!" And she was outside, closing the door on Patrolman John Joseph Swazey's shining face.

He returned to his chair, tilted it back against the wall and contemplated the future with a happy smile. "Dames," he told himself philosophically, "are funny. But deep down underneath, they're all alike. You just gotta know how to handle them."

Instead of taking her out of the red door and down the stoop, Janie's feet for some reason she couldn't explain took her upstairs.

At Mae Wells' door she stopped and listened. There were voices from within, a woman's and a man's. The woman's voice was Mae's; the man's was new to her.

She sighed with relief. She had been afraid that it might be Johnny's.

If anyone had told her she was eavesdropping she would have been shocked. Nice girls don't go listening at other people's doors—not normally. But Janie's condition was far from normal.

For the first time in her life she was in love up to the hilt. And for the first time her mating instinct had been aroused to the full. And for the first time she felt the need to fight for her man.

Rather a formidable list of firsts. Under such conditions almost anything can happen to almost any girl—and usually does.

Somehow those unmanageable feet of Janie's were taking her up another flight to Johnny's door. Why? She certainly didn't intend to make up with him. No, indeed. He'd have to come crawling and begging first, and give a very good explanation of his affair with that hussy.

No, she would not go into Johnny's. She climbed another flight to the Andersons, and rang their bell.

Mrs. Anderson came to the door and looked out astigmatically. "Oh, it's you." She turned her head inward. "It's the girl from this morning, Lucius," she called. "The tall blonde one. Not that other." She added, "Come in, come in. Lucius and I were just discussing the murder. We have a theory. Come in and see what you think of it."

The room was furnished with uncomfortable wicker furniture. On a table was a copy of "The Brooklyn Tablet" and Jan Valtin's "Out of the Night." The seat Jane took felt as uncomfortable as it looked.

"Isn't it exciting," gushed Mrs. Anderson. "Having a murder right in your own house. But I forgot—you don't live here, do you? You were staying with that boy downstairs."

"Just calling for him," Jane amended.

"Well, he's a nice boy. So Aryan looking, isn't he?"

"He's pretty nice," Jane agreed. "What's your theory about the murder?"

"I think," said Mrs. Anderson, and her voice sank to a whisper, "that it's more than just a plain murder." She paused for effect.

"Why?" asked Janie, and she found herself whispering, too.

"I don't know. I just feel it. I was saying to Lucius only yesterday, I said 'Mark my words, Lucius, they'll stop at nothing to get their way. Not even murder!' Didn't I, Lucius?"

She didn't wait for his automatic, "Yes, dear," but ran on. "And no sooner were the words out of my mouth than it happened. The murder, I mean. You can't convince me that they're not behind it. They'd stoop to anything."

"Who are 'they'?" Jane demanded excitedly.

"Come now," said Mrs. Anderson, "don't tell me you don't know what's going on."

Jane's excitement was mounting. "Honest," she said, "I haven't the slightest idea of what you're talking about. Please tell me."

"You mean to say you don't know about the plot to take over the country?"

Jane shook her head. "I've heard something about a fifth column, but—"

"Fifth column, fiddlesticks," snorted Mrs. Anderson. "The only fifth column we have is right in the White House! He and his crew of Communists! You can mark my word they're behind this murder somehow."

Jane had been holding her breath with suspense. Now it came out in a rush. She felt very flat.

Mr. Anderson said, "They're Jews."

"Exactly!" Mrs. Anderson rushed on. "They're ruining the country. Look what they did to our boys. Started a whole war just so that they'd have an excuse to send our boys to Russia to learn how to be Reds."

"Whoa?" said Janie. "You're getting me mixed up. I thought it was Hitler and the Japanese who started the war."

"Piffle!" cried Mrs. Anderson. "That's just newspaper talk. They have to say that or they'll be censored."

Jane realized quickly that to argue the point would be fruitless. "It's a very interesting theory," she said. "But I'm sure Mr. Roosevelt didn't do this job personally. If we could find the man who did the shooting and make him confess who had sent him, we might be able to prove your theory."

"Exactly what I was telling Lucius just before you rang the bell. Lucius doesn't agree with me, but he's such a baby about these things. You know who I suspect? Mr. Ponds! He doesn't give enough hot water for one thing."

"But what in the world has Mr. Ponds got to do with it? He isn't a Communist or a Jew, is he?"

"My dear—" started Mr. Anderson.

His wife ignored him. "You never can tell. Didn't you ever notice what a big nose he has?"

"No. But even if he has. The man was killed with a gun, not a nose."

Mrs. Anderson put on a righteous look. "If I was the sort of person who tells everything she knows I could say a few things—"

"My dear!" cried Mr. Anderson in an alarmed tone.

"Don't you shout at me, Lucius Anderson," his wife snapped. "My dear—my dear! Every time I open my mouth, he starts my dearing all over the place. It's revolting."

Lucius had shriveled up like a beaten hound. "I just wanted to say," he began, but that's as far as he got.

"*He* wanted to say! When I want to say something he says 'my dear!' Now he wants to say. Well, I'll tell you right now, Lucius Anderson, that I won't be bullied. Now you be quiet and don't interrupt. Where was I?"

"You were telling me about Mr. Ponds."

"Oh, yes. Well—here's what the police don't know. Mr. Ponds lied to them. He said he wasn't home all afternoon and he was!"

"But my dear—" Mr. Anderson sounded agitated.

Mrs. Anderson ignored him.

"He was?" Janie was beginning to get excited. "How do you know?"

"Because." Mrs. Anderson looked around the small apartment to make sure no one was listening. "I saw him myself!"

Janie shook her head in an attempt to clear it. "But you couldn't have," she said. "You went right from shopping to meet your husband at the restaurant."

"My dear, I insist—" Mr. Anderson might have been alone for all the attention he received.

"And carry all those packages with me? Nonsense!" Mrs. Anderson answered. "I stopped off to drop them at home first. That's when I saw Mr. Ponds. He looked very suspicious, too, I can tell you."

"Why didn't you tell that to Mr. MacWilliams?"

"And have them arrest Mr. Ponds? Then we'd get no hot water at all! But if he's an agent of 'theirs' that's different. Then I'll tell—what do you think?"

Janie scratched her head. "I'm not sure," she said. "Maybe you're right. But on the other hand, I understand that the murdered man had a simply tremendous nose. So perhaps he was the Red agent, and the one who killed him was on our side."

Mrs. Anderson put her hand to her mouth. "I hadn't thought of that," she said. "But it's possible. Oh, my goodness, I don't know what to do now. Must you go?" she asked as Janie made for the door.

"Yes. Sorry. I'll see you again. Good-bye."

Outside Janie wanted to spit. She was filled with disgust. She had heard about people like the Andersons, but this was her first close up experience. She felt dirty, inside and out.

On the floor below she stopped at Johnny's door. "Well, I'm in the house," she told her inquiring self impatiently. "I can at least find out if he's been let out of jail."

She tried Johnny's door. It was locked. She felt under the door mat. The key was there. She opened the door, returned the key to its hiding place, went inside and slammed the door after her.

Even the Chinese red door looked good to Johnny Angel. It had no bars on it. As he walked up the steps toward it, he felt a strange little tug at his hat. It felt as though someone had dropped something on it from above.

He took the hat off. There was nothing on the brim, but there were two neat little holes through the crown. He looked at them curiously. "Now how in the world did they get there?" he wondered.

He proceeded up the steps. He was three steps from the top when the thought struck him. "That tug—those holes! They're bullet holes! Somebody just took a shot at me!" He took the last three steps in one terrified jump. A second later he was behind the protective panels of the ugly red door. His nerves were as taut as violin strings. His legs turned rubbery.

As he went up the stairs he was sure he had heard his apartment door closing. He proceeded cautiously. He listened at the door. Yes, there were footsteps inside. This was too much. Bullets outside. Inside marauders and perhaps more bullets. He turned the knob slowly, being sure not to make any noise. This time he wasn't going to wait for Whisper to attack. He was going to do the attacking. His sore face cried out for revenge.

It was dark inside, but he could make out someone moving across the bedroom toward the light. He didn't wait. He took two running steps and launched himself through the air. His shoulder hit a body amidships, bore it down with him. He was on top, the marauder underneath!

The figure underneath gave an unexpected squeal and subsided. The fight was much easier than he had expected. He held his captive down firmly and used his hands for eyes. He felt the face, body, hair. It was long hair.

"My God!" he said aloud. "It's a woman!"

Jane said, "Oh, Johnny! I was so afraid. I thought it was one of those gangsters." Her very voice made a new man out of Johnny. He forgot how miserable he had been feeling. "So did I. Did I hurt you?"

"I don't know. I feel as though I was ruined. What did you hit me with? You certainly have a masterful way about you."

"Gosh, it's good to find you here. I just got out of jail. I was going to wash up and go looking for you."

Suddenly Janie remembered that she was angry at him. "Are you sure you wouldn't have preferred your red-head tonight?" she demanded coolly.

"Listen, Janie." He rolled her over and folded her in his arms. "You've got to believe me. That redhead doesn't mean anything to me. I never even spoke to her but once before this morning. I swear it.

"Oh, if I could only believe you."

"You can. I wouldn't lie to you, Janie. I love you too much."

"But she called you honey."

"Darling, you don't understand. She calls everybody honey. It doesn't mean anything."

Janie sighed. Her lips parted as though to speak, but no words came. Finally she whispered, "Kiss me, Johnny."

Johnny had just kissed her when the bell rang. They jumped up. Jane snapped on the light and went to the window where she stood cooling her flaming cheeks.

Johnny called, "Just a minute," wiped the rouge off his lips with his handkerchief and went to the door.

It was Sam Isherman, keeping his appointment.

CHAPTER 5

A few minutes later the bell rang again and Sam Isherman said: "That's probably Bill Lawrence. I invited him over. Good head on him. Maybe he can help us figure this out."

It was the iron-jawed local chairman. They went into the living room and sat down.

Jane felt a little out of place with these three men. Unions represented something she did not understand and therefore resented a little. Before she had awakened to the fact that she loved Johnny Angel, her antagonism had been stronger. Now there was the unconscious thought that if his union meant so much to him there must be something good in it.

She looked at Johnny. Sitting with these other men, his face seemed changed. Yes, it was just as boyish and lovable as ever. But there was a subtle difference about him that was hard to define.

It may have been that his jaw was a little stiffer, or his lips were a little firmer—she couldn't be sure just what it was. But suddenly she had the feeling that this man, in whose arms she had so willingly reposed just a few minutes before, was a stranger to her.

Did she know him? She only knew the after work Johnny who was tall and handsome and lots of fun. This was a new Johnny, a serious, forceful Johnny with an intentness which was overwhelming.

Sam Isherman was talking. "Now, if we compare notes we may be able to fit some of these pieces together. I for one have some important news. The gun that you took from the Runt, Johnny, did not kill Angell!"

"Did not?"

"No. The police are positive of it."

Something clicked in Jane's mind. "Then that changes every-thing!" she cried. "I thought it wasn't important, but it is."

"What is?"

"Why, about Mrs. Anderson and Mr. Ponds."

They looked at her expectantly.

"Don't you understand? I just thought the Andersons were Christian Fronters, and very stupid people. But if the two gunmen didn't kill Mr. Angell, then it could have been Mrs. Anderson or Mr. Ponds."

Johnny shook his head. "They couldn't have, Janie. They weren't there."

"But, of course they were. She said so herself!"

"Will you stop talking in riddles, Janie. Who said what?"

"Oh, how silly," Janie giggled. "I forgot you didn't know about my interview with Mrs. Anderson. She—Mrs. Anderson—told me that Mr. Ponds had been at home at the time of the murder. She knew because she had been home herself and had seen him."

"That," said Sam Isherman, "is what I call a fine piece of detective work."

Bill Lawrence nodded warmly.

Johnny, who was sitting next to her, squeezed her hand.

Janie found herself liking these men more than she had.

"But it also makes things a little more complicated, by bringing in two new suspects. At first it seemed like a simple case of rounding up the two gunmen. Now it's broadening out. Besides, Whisper and the Runt seem to have lit out. The cops have had a dragnet out for them without any results, so far."

"I don't think they've gone very far," said Johnny.

"Why not?" asked Sam.

Johnny got up, went outside and brought back his hat. He threw it to Isherman.

"Whew," the lawyer whistled as he saw the neat little holes. "When did that happen?"

"About a half hour ago. One of those two were waiting for me downstairs."

"Didn't miss by much. Did you see him?"

"No. I ducked inside."

"Well—it might have been one of them, but on the other hand—it might have been almost anyone else."

It was clear that they had no way of identifying the shooter.

Janie looked at the holes and felt her blood running cold. She wanted to take Johnny in her arms and mother him. He had missed death by inches, and she had thought only of her own petty jealousy.

"About this code," said Isherman. "All afternoon I've been trying to make something out of it. No luck." He had taken it from his pocket. They each took a chance at trying to make sense out of the strange array of figures, but no one had any more success than the lawyer.

Johnny grinned. "MacWilliams would love to have that," he said. "I told him I'd lost it."

"Tch, tch," said Sam. "It's not smart, Johnny, to lie to the police that way."

"Well, I don't like him," said Johnny flatly. "He's just the kind of a cop who goes out breaking up picket lines for his own amusement."

"Maybe so, Johnny. But remember, this isn't a strike—it's a murder. This time we're in a position where we and the cops are working together."

"Just the same," said Johnny stubbornly, "since we hadn't said anything about the code so far, you shouldn't have told MacWilliams about it."

Isherman stared at him for a moment. "Let me get this straight, Johnny. You think I told him—"

"Sure. Didn't you?"

"Why did you think I told him, Johnny?"

"Because I didn't and nobody else knew about it but the four of us in this room."

"I see." Isherman nodded contemplatively. He turned to Jane. "Did you mention it to anyone?"

"No."

"How about you, Bill?"

Bill Lawrence shook his head. "Not me."

Sam sighed. "Well, that makes another problem. Because I never mentioned that code."

"Then how would MacWilliams know?"

"That," said Isherman, "is the problem."

"Perhaps," Jane offered, "they lied to you about the gunmen. Perhaps they caught them. They knew about it."

"Could be," said Isherman.

"There's another possibility," said Bill Lawrence. They turned to him. "As I understand it, young Hirdler knew about the code. Maybe he told MacWilliams."

They digested that for a moment. "Possible but highly improbable," was the general verdict.

"I think," said Janie, "that we ought to turn all the code messages over to the police. It might help them."

Isherman and Lawrence agreed with her, but Johnny was doubtful. "I tell you, I don't trust MacWilliams," he insisted. "But," he swung around to Janie, "what do you mean by 'all the messages?' We only have one."

She pulled the others out of her bag. "I found these in the apartment downstairs."

All three looked at her incredulously as she told of her dealings with Detective Swazey. "He's going to be waiting for me at twelve," she teased Johnny. "I'm supposed to meet him."

"You'll do nothing of the kind."

"Hold on, Johnny," Bill Lawrence said. "It might be a good thing."

"Good for whom—Swazey?"

"No—for us. Swazey's on MacWilliams' staff. Perhaps Jane can get some inside dope from him. She seems to have a gift for finding out things."

"But I had no intention—" Jane was flustered. Actually meeting Swazey had been furthest from her thoughts.

Sam Isherman chimed in, taking Bill Lawrence's side.

"But I remind him of Edna," Jane wailed. "His old girl who just acted like an iceberg, but was really a volcano underneath."

No one but Johnny had any doubts that she could handle Swazey without any difficulty. Johnny was overruled. He wasn't happy about it.

"Now that that's settled, let's see what we can make of these other puzzles," said Isherman. "First—why should anyone shoot a man and then cut one of his hands off?"

"Fingerprints?" suggested Jane.

"No—one hand can identify him as easily as two."

"A ring on one of his fingers?"

Johnny said, "No—it would have been simpler to cut the finger off."

They mulled over it, but could find no satisfactory answer.

"All right," Isherman said. "We'll let that rest. What's the answer to this one. Why was Angell at the H.A. plant the day he was killed?"

"I can try to get the answer to that," said Johnny. "I know Ethel, the receptionist in the front office. I'll talk to her. Everyone who comes in goes through her."

"Is she a red-head by any chance?" asked Jane offensively.

"No, but what's the difference? I'm just going to talk to her."

"Humpf." Jane would not be appeased. "You certainly do talk around a lot."

"Come on, kids. This is no time for love spats," said Sam Isherman.

Bill Lawrence said: "If it'll keep peace in the family, I'll try to pump Ethel. We're pretty good friends."

Jane felt a little ashamed of herself. Suddenly it seemed very important that these friends of Johnny should like her. They were important people, doing important work and she was behaving like a school-kid.

"What about these codes?" said Sam. "I vote that we turn them over to MacWilliams."

"But first we make copies," insisted Johnny. "I want to try my hand at them."

"All right," said Sam. "We can give him the originals in the morning. Meanwhile you, Bill, will check on Angell at the plant, and Jane will find out whatever she can about MacWilliams. And all of you be careful. Remember, there's someone around with a gun and a careless trigger finger."

Jane looked at her watch. "I'd better go if I'm going to catch Swazey," she said. With female inconsistency, she gave Johnny a peck on the ear and was off.

Bill and Sam said their good nights and followed her down the steps.

She waited until they had left the house, then knocked gently at the door of the first floor apartment.

John Joseph Swazey opened the door.

"Ready?" she asked.

"Waiting for my relief. He should be here any minute. Come in."

"No, it wouldn't look nice."

"Maybe you're right. Where'll you be?"

"I'll wait outside."

"O.K." Swazey was beaming. As he closed the door he hummed a few bars from "Happy Days Are Here Again."

Jane started up to Johnny's apartment. She had decided that she owed him an apology for her meanness over the Ethel situation. Now was as good a time as any to do it.

As her head cleared the floor above she saw a man go into Mae Wells' apartment. The man was John Angel.

Jane's mouth closed with a snap. She turned and went down the stairs.

Outside on the stoop she talked to herself in a low monotone. Anyone who heard her would have been amazed. Ladies aren't supposed to know such words—much less use them.

In a little while Officer Swazey came out and Jane walked away with him—still fuming.

CHAPTER 6

Mae Wells had a form-fitting housecoat on.

Housecoats are a peculiar phenomenon. They use more material than two ordinary dresses. They droop gracefully to the floor and conceal far more of their wearer than any other type of apparel. Ladies in housecoats don't even have feet, not to speak of legs.

In spite of all these factors which should make the housecoat the emblem of puritanism, this deceitful garment might just as well have S-E-X embroidered down its front in big red letters.

Mae Wells' housecoat fitted snugly around well-turned hips and the upper section seemed to come directly from a picture in *Esquire*.

Mae's face, with art work completed and topped by an upslung coiffure of burning curls wasn't a thing to be easily ignored, either.

Johnny gulped.

Mae smiled and said, "I'm glad you decided to visit." She used just the right amount of coyness mixed with the proper proportion of the friendly "hello, neighbor" line.

Johnny quivered and pulled his eyes from Mae's lips to the tips of her mules as they shyly stuck out beneath the housecoat. He wet his lips and said, "It's not a—exactly a visit."

Mae's eyes opened innocently. Half pouting, she held out her arms invitingly. But Johnny proved that he had the stuff of which heroes are made—heroes who could hold their positions in the face of extreme provocation—by standing up and walking to the window. Then looking safely out at the traffic lights on Seventh Avenue, he said: "I can only stay a minute. I wanted to talk to you about the—the murder."

"Oh!" Mae really was nice about it. She put her arms down and took the pout off her lips and the invitation out of her eyes, and when Johnny turned to her again she looked very demure and quite interested in what he had on his mind.

"Where do I fit in?"

"I'm not sure. Unless you know either Mr. Ponds or the Andersons."

"Ponds? Well—all I know about him is that he comes for the rent on the first. Never misses. But the Andersons are something else again. He's a nice old guy, but she wears the pants. Every time I've met him alone he's smiled and been friendly, but when he's with her, he looks right past me. Just what do you want me to find out? If I can get him alone for a while, I'll worm it out of him."

"That's the stuff! You get him and see what you can find out. They know more than they've told. We've found out that both Ponds and Mr. Anderson were in the house at the time of the murder."

Mae whistled. "That's pretty serious, isn't it?" she asked. Then, "Do you think I ought to see him like this?" She made a gesture indicating her housecoat.

Johnny nodded admiringly.

Mae raised an eyebrow. "It doesn't seem to have much effect on you," she said.

"Oh, doesn't it, though," said Johnny. "If you only knew the half of it! G'bye!" He was at the door in a hurried retreat. "I'll check with you tomorrow," he called over his shoulder as he dashed to the safety of the hall.

Mae looked at herself in her mirror and smiled a little sadly. "Either," she said to the voluptuous figure in the glass, "you're losing your grip, or the boy is really awfully deep in love with that long-legged blonde."

She sat thinking for a moment. How to get Mr. Anderson alone. That was the problem. Obviously she couldn't knock at his door—not now, anyway— for Mrs. Anderson might be at home and that would crab everything.

Footsteps on the stairs. She rushed to the door. Ah—the reward of virtue—here was Mr. Anderson himself, dutifully coming home to his waiting spouse.

She made sure that her eyes were blank and harmless as she met him in the hall. No use scaring him. He might run.

"Mr.—er—Anderson?"

He stopped, smiled benignly. "Yes, my dear?"

"I wonder if you would mind helping me. The window in my bedroom is stuck. I've tried and tried, but I just can't get it open." She made a helpless gesture. "It's so hard not having a man in the house. Men can do so many things that we poor women can't."

Mr. Anderson's chest grew several inches larger. "Why, of course, my dear." He followed her in.

"I've been asking Mr. Ponds to fix it for weeks," said Mae, truthfully enough, "but he's so busy he never seems to get around to it. And I just can't sleep without my window open, can you?"

"No, indeed," he agreed. "Is this the one?"

"Yes, that's it."

He put his hands on the ledge and pushed. Nothing happened. He spread his feet and pushed harder. Nothing happened. He screwed his neck sideways and examined the offending frame. "Looks like some paint stuck in there."

He made a fist and used it to hammer all around the frame. Then he braced himself and gave one powerful push. This should do it.

But it didn't. The window didn't budge.

Mr. Anderson's face was a little red from the combination of annoyance and exertion.

Mae handed him a hammer. "Perhaps this would help," she said.

He took it silently and returned to the window.

She slipped into the kitchen and poured some ginger ale into a tall glass. Then she added a stiff jigger of whiskey. She brought it into the bedroom and set it unostentatiously on the table.

The combination of hammer, fist and muscular endeavor won out over the stubbornness of the window frame. It went up with a crash which was completely unexpected and Mr. Anderson had to pull himself back quickly to keep from tumbling out.

"Oh, Mr. Anderson. You're wonderful! How can I ever thank you!"

"It's nothing, my dear. Nothing at all," he puffed.

"Oh, but it is. No use trying to pass it off so lightly. It was very nice of you to do it for me. Please sit down until you get your breath back."

She eased him into a chair. "I—uh—have to be going," he mumbled uncomfortably. "My uh—wife you know—"

"Now, isn't that just like a man," Mae pouted a little. "He gets all over exerted to help me out and then won't even wait to cool off. Why, what would your wife think if you came in all red and perspiring like that? No! It wouldn't do at all. Now you just sit there a few minutes until you cool off—and here—here's a nice cool drink. That'll help you." She put the glass into his unresisting hand. "You drink that. I'll get another for myself."

She went out and made herself a drink. When she came back Mr. Anderson's glass was empty. "My, you were thirsty. Wait—I'll get you another." This time she put in a double dose of whiskey.

Mr. Anderson drank it with evident enjoyment, loosening up noticeably as he drank. Mae watched the metamorphosis with a bit of surprise. You have a right to expect some change in a man after a few drinks, but this miniature Jekyl—Hyde transformation was a little more than she had bargained for.

The almost ministerial smile which Mr. Anderson had worn when he entered changed until it was practically a leer. His nose which might well have been painted blue before, now suddenly developed a set of quivering, dilating nostrils. And his eyes had changed entirely. There was a light in them now which had been entirely lacking. This was no longer Mrs. Anderson's husband. Here was a man in his own right and each sip made him more so.

He looked around the room as though seeing it for the first time. He shook his head approvingly and said, "Nice place you've got here."

Mae nodded her agreement comfortably. Let the victim talk, was her motto.

"Good liquor, too." He looked at his empty glass significantly.

"Sure—but it's the kind that sneaks up on you."

She made no move to refill his glass.

"Sneak up on me? Why I can drink a quart and never even show it. But my wife, now, she doesn't like me to drink. Says I talk too much. What does she know about it? That old bat!"

He put his hand to his mouth and for a second signs of the meek mousy man returned, but the liquor proved stronger than his inhibitions, for a second later he repeated his brash words.

"Yes, a bat! An ugly old bat, that's what she is. Always holding me down. I'm going up and tell her right now. She's nothing but an old bat."

He began to get out of his chair.

Mae hastily pushed him back. "Why do that? She wouldn't understand. Here, have another drink and tell me about it. I can understand you." Better to risk getting him tight than to let him get away.

Anderson sighed, took the drink and sat hack. "Always belittling," he complained. "Always taking all the credit. But who has the brains, I'm asking you? Who? Me, that's who! Do you know what I did?"

"What?"

"I organized the whole neighborhood into our club myself. But when they got together, who was made the president? My wife! Who wrote her speeches? Mel Why, if it wasn't for me, she'd forget all about the Jews. She always does!"

"Why is that?"

"Because all she can see is Communists. She doesn't understand that the Commies are just another Jew organization, like the banks and—and—and the President and all the rest."

He relapsed into morose silence.

"It's easy to see that she'd be lost without you," Mae prompted.

"Lost is right. It was me explained that we had to connect with all the other patriotic groups. I made the contact with the Camelias and the Crusaders and the Cops and the—"

"The cops? Are the cops in it, too?"

He looked at her surprisedly. "Didn't you know? Oh, not all of them. Just a few. But they're mighty helpful. They know how to handle Jews all right—and Commies, too."

"It must be wonderful," said Mae, "to be the brains behind such an important organization."

"Important isn't the word. Vital! That's it. We're going to save the country from Jew Bolshevism, we are."

"How marvelous! I wish I could help. But how can you do it? You'd need guns and things, wouldn't you?"

"We can do it all right. They did it in Germany, didn't they? No Jews there! And don't you worry about guns. We've got them, too."

"You think of everything!"

"You said it. But shh!" He put his finger to his lips in an exaggerated gesture. "Don't tell anybody about the guns. Ponds wouldn't like it."

"Ponds did you say?"

"Sure, Ponds!" He pointed downward toward the landlord's apartment, and winked heavily. "That's where they are. He's the, shh, the Keeper of the Arms." He blinked knowingly, like a boiled owl, and sank back in his chair.

Mae thought he was falling asleep when suddenly he thrust his finger out and said loudly, "Doesn't that prove it?"

"Prove what?"

"My wife."

"Oh—your wife."

"Yeah—that know it all old bat. Why, she doesn't even know about Ponds. Nobody knows it. Nobody but me. And I'm not going to tell. No sir. Never. The ugly old bat."

He sank back again and began to snore. This time he really was asleep.

Mae sat looking at him, mulling over what he had said. No, it wasn't exactly the information Johnny had asked for—but it would do. Yes, indeed—it would do.

CHAPTER 7

"What's the matter, babe? You upset about something?" asked Officer John Joseph Swazey as he swung down the street with Jane on his arm.

She forced a smile. "Oh, no. Nothing at all. It'd be nice if you wouldn't hold my arm so protectively. Someone might notice and get the wrong idea."

"I get it," he laughed uproariously. "Might think it was a pinch." He dropped her arm. "Anything to oblige a babe like you. Where'd you like to go?"

"Well, let's think. How about—"

"You live near here, babe?"

"Yes. How about going to—"

"How's about going to your house?"

That pulled her up short. "My house?"

"Sure. We can pick up a bottle and sit and talk friendly and quiet like. Unless—say—you ain't one of them babes that lives with her mother—are you?"

"No."

"Girlfriend?"

"No."

"Uh—boyfriend, by any chance?"

"No!" snappishly. "I live alone."

"Fine!" chortled Joe. What are we waiting for? I figured you for a dame with your own layout!"

"But I don't usually entertain strange men at my apartment."

"Strange men! Who's a strange man? I ain't strange. I'm John Joseph Swazey, remember? And you and me are going to be swell friends. Besides, what's the harm in it? We'll just talk and kind of get better acquainted."

"Like you and Edna used to do, hey?"

"Gosh, you sure are like her. She was some wonderful girl. Wait here a minute, will you? I'll pop in and get a bottle. Got any preference? I like gin."

Jane shuddered. "No gin," she said.

"What then? Rye? Scotch? Irish?"

"Anything at all but gin."

"O.K., babe."

In a few minutes he was out and they were walking again, a square-necked package which promised Mount Vernon under his arm.

"What have you got against gin?"

"It was the first thing I ever drank and it made me sick—awfully sick. The smell of it still turns my stomach."

He nodded. "Edna was the same way. But with her it was Bourbon. As for me—two drinks of rum will knock me heels over high water. Got any sody water at home or should we pick some up?"

"I have some," she answered. "But wait a minute. I haven't agreed to go to my house. In fact—"

"Aw, come on, babe. Don't be a crab. What you got to worry about? You can take care of yourself, can't you?"

She cocked a quizzical eye at him. "I wonder just how you mean that, but the answer is yes—I can take care of myself."

She looked at him, thinking. The memory of Johnny entering Mae's apartment hit her again. "Why not?" she demanded as though the idea was hers originally. "Why not, indeed? What's sauce for the goose— Come on, friend Swazey. We're going home."

Her long, slender legs rapped along the pavement so quickly that Swazey had to hurry to keep up with her. He smiled a self-satisfied smile.

She opened her door with her latchkey and he followed her into the attractive band box of an apartment.

She waved an arm to the kitchenette. "You'll find soda and ice cubes in the refrigerator. Glasses in the cupboard up above. You get started. I've got a few minutes of work to do first."

"On your story?"

"Story? Oh, yes. But it won't take long."

"Let me help."

"No. You prepare the drinks. I can work better alone."

She took the typewriter into the bedroom, pulled the code messages out of her bag and quickly made copies. She folded the copies, went into the bathroom and put them into the cache with the original code message.

When she re-entered the living room, Swazey was sitting in an easy chair with his coat off, sipping a long drink. Another amber-filled glass sat on the table waiting for her.

Janie took her drink and sat down. Then she put on her prettiest smile.

"O.K. John Joseph. Now talk to me. I've always wanted to know about detectives. Fascinating business, isn't it?"

"Aw—it ain't so much," said John Joseph. "In fact, I'll tell you a secret. It's a little boring."

"Now you're just being modest," said Jane. "After all, murder may not be pretty but it's certainly exciting."

"Yeah—in a way. But it's mostly routine work."

"You mean all these books I've been reading are—"

"Books—bah. Bunk. I'd like to see some of those wise mystery writers try to catch a killer. Hah. That's a laugh."

"I don't know." Jane felt herself called on to defend the noble art of mystery writing. "After all—"

"You said it, babe. You don't know. Look." Swazey was warming to his subject—one which he seemed to relish only second to Edna. "Take all these killings in the books. Does a mug ever go out and shoot someone plain and simple the way they do in real life? Oh, no. Nothing like that. They have to do it fancy like."

"But some cases are unusual, aren't they?" asked Jane. "This Angell case, for instance. It's not usual for a murdered man to have a hand chopped off, is it?"

"No, but we'll find out why it was done. And when we do find out, it'll be for some very usual reason. Then take the phony detectives in the books. All kinds of guys are detectives; psychologists, doctors, professors, old ladies—everything but honest to goodness detectives. And even when they do use a cop in the story, how does he do his work? Always by tricks. Never the good old routine work or the stool pigeons."

"Stool pigeons?"

"Sure—most of our work is done through stool pigeons. If we get a line on those two gunmen in this case how do you think we'll do it? Through some rat who brings in the information so that he can keep in right himself."

Jane shuddered. "Disgusting, isn't it?"

"Yeah—and boring, like I was saying."

"All detectives don't feel that way, do they? This MacWilliams, now. Your boss. He seems to get some pleasure out of hounding people."

"Oh, him!" And Swazey dismissed his boss with a broad gesture.

"What do you mean, 'oh, him'?"

"He hates everybody. So this business is good for him. Gives him a chance to browbeat people."

"Why does he hate everybody?"

"Why talk about MacWilliams? It's enough I have to look at him all day. Let's talk about something interesting. Let's talk about you— and here, let me fill your glass again."

"But I'd like to talk about MacWilliams. I like to know what makes people like him tick."

Swazey chortled. "That's a good word for the boss, all right. He's sure a ticker, he is. But as for me, I'm more interested in how you tick. You know you got a gorgeous figure?"

"You really think so?" Jane was half serious. "I've been told it's a little too much on the boyish side."

"And what's wrong with a boyish figure?" demanded John Joseph. "Boyish figures are the style now, babe, but I liked 'em even when they weren't."

"You're just trying to make me feel good, John Joseph."

"Nah, nothing of the sort. I go for your type, babe. The callipygian cuties for me."

"Is that respectable, or are you insulting me in some foreign language?"

"Hah, hah!" Swazey roared. "That always gets a rise out of them. But I should think a newspaper gal could understand English!"

"What does it mean—that calla—something or other?"

"Callipygian, babe. Check it in the dictionary."

"I will and right now, too. And if it's not something nice I'll—"

"Oh, it's nice all right."

She pulled down her Webster and was thumbing through the pages. The words seemed a little blurred, but Janie attributed it to tiredness. She never gave a thought to the liquor she had been consuming while talking to Swazey. "Here it is," she called. "Now, let's see. Callipygian. Having—well—shaped—thighs and— Well, I like that," she began indignantly.

"So do I, babe." Swazey was right behind her, breathing heavily on her neck.

Jane waved a restraining hand in front of his face. "Take it easy, brother. Sit down and cool off. Remember, I'm not Edna. I'm a much more talkative gal and I feel like talking."

"But—"

"No buts. You don't want to spoil our beautiful friendship before it even gets started, do you? Of course not. So just sit down and be a good boy and talk to me."

Swazey's face had a look of chagrin on it, so Jane felt she had better not be too drastic in her orders.

"Just have patience, John Joseph. Remember, I only met you tonight and it takes time for me to overcome my shyness."

Swazey, reassured as to her friendly attitude, grinned. "O.K., babe. You may be hard to get, but you're worth waiting for."

He flopped back into his chair. "What'll we talk about, pigeon?"

Janie took a surreptitious look at herself in the mirror as she walked back to her seat.

"Let's talk about this murder," she said to Swazey. "Remember, I've got to get a story out of it. If I can get enough dope on it I may be able to stretch it out into a series. One article on the murdered man, one on MacWilliams, one on you, of course, and maybe another one taking in all the suspects. So tell me about that."

"Sure—what do you want to know?" Swazey asked, and refilled the glasses again.

"Well, let's start with the suspects. What about them?"

"O.K. First on the list ought to be the two gunmen. Young feller living above Angell claims he was stuck up by two gangsters the day of the killing. Name of Angel. Might have been mistaken for Angell. Corroborative evidence—his gal backs him up. She was over at his house when he was nabbed. Living with him, I guess—"

"She is not!" Jane exploded.

"No? How do you know? Interview her?"

"Yes," answered Jane, more coolly. "I spoke to her this afternoon. What about the gunmen? I heard they had been picked up."

"Naw." Swazey shook his head. "You got a wrong steer there. We haven't even been able to get a smell of them, yet. MacWilliams doesn't like them as suspects, anyway."

"No? Who does he like?"

"The young feller living upstairs. Angel. He'd like to pin it on him."
"Why?"

"Oh, I don't know. That's MacWilliams. This Angel seems to be some high mucky muck in his union, and MacWilliams just don't like unions."

"But he wouldn't railroad an innocent man because—"

"Wouldn't he though? You don't know MacWilliams."

"But why does he hate unions so?"

Swazey shrugged his shoulders. "He says they're un-American."
"Are they?"

"Heck, no. Before I joined the force I worked in an auto plant for a coupla years. We had a union, a good one, too. Did plenty for the men. And today it's doing plenty for the war. But that doesn't change Mac's feelings."

"But to push an innocent man around—"

"That's nothing for Mac. Remember when those Christian Fronters were tried for conspiracy—they had guns and bullets stored away?"

Jane nodded.

"Well, I'm willing to bet that MacWilliams helped them get the stuff!"

"Nothing like that came out in the trial."

"No, he keeps himself too well covered. But I'll bet on it just the same."

"If you're so sure why didn't you say something about it?"

He stared at her wide-eyed. "You crazy, babe? They'd break me before I could get my full name on an affidavit. You can't buck your boss in this kind of a set-up. But let's forget about MacWilliams for a while. Talk about you for a change. How come a dainty morsel like you hasn't been gobbled up long before this? Why don't—"

"No, no," Janie cut in. "We're talking about the murder, not about me. You said before that you'd probably find some ordinary reason for the man's hand being cut off. Now I've been trying to think of ordinary reasons for it and I can't for the life of me. Put that brain of yours to it and let's see what comes out."

"Well—I hadn't thought about it much," said Swazey, "but the way to figure out a thing like that is to put yourself in the place of the murderer. I'll be the murderer, see? You're Angell. All right!"

He got out of his chair and advanced toward her. "I put my gun next to your head and pull the trigger." He used his forefinger in place of a gun.

"Boom. All right. You're dead. Now I clean out your pockets. Umm—nice little pockets."

Janie pushed his hands away. "Hey, cut it out. Stick to the murder. Were his pockets empty when he was found?"

"Umm," Swazey sighed. "All right. Back to work. Yep. The pockets were empty. So now what? Now I'm going to cut your hand off at the wrist."

"But why?" asked Janie.

"Yeah—that's the question—why?" Swazey scratched his head. "Maybe we better do it all over again. Maybe I missed something."

"No, thanks," said Jane. "You didn't miss a thing."

"But he must have had a reason for cutting that hand off," said John Joseph.

"Well, at least we agree on one point. But what was the reason?"

"Wait. I better have another drink to loosen up my mind."

He refilled the glasses. The bottle was less than half full now. Jane noticed it wonderingly. Where in the world had all that whiskey gone? They just couldn't have drunk that much. Why, she didn't even feel high. A little warm perhaps, but her mind was as sharp as a whistle. Just the same, perhaps she had better take it easy from now on. Liquor had a way of hitting all of a sudden.

Swazey was talking, she realized.

"Maybe it was one of those black hand organizations. Or doesn't that make sense?"

Jane shook her head.

"No, it doesn't. First place, there is no more black hand. Second place, even when there was they didn't cut hands off."

"No?"

"No!"

"All right. We'll figure something else." Swazey's voice was getting a little thick.

Jane noticed it. She pointed an accusing finger at him. "You," she said as a school teacher might say to a student, "are getting drunk!"

"Me, drunk? Not me. I'm sober as a judge."

"You are too," Jane insisted, "getting drunk. Inebriated. Intoxicated. Plastered. Stinko. Whoosh."

"Aw, I am not. Come on, let's figure out this arm business."

"What arm business?"

"Angell's arm."

"He didn't have an arm. It was a hand."

"All right—hand. What happened to it? Maybe the killer saves hands for souvenirs."

"No," said Jane. "No, not that."

"Why not?"

"If he's saving hands, why didn't he take both?"

"Maybe he only saves left hands. These collectors are queer, you know."

Jane giggled.

"What's funny?" Swazey demanded.

"I knew a collector once," she confided.

"Yeah? What did he collect?"

"Garbage," she announced solemnly.

He looked at her owlishly. "Babe," he decided, "*you're* the one who's getting drunk."

"I am not. I'm soberer than you. Here, I'll show you," and exercising great care she walked straight down the line of the rug without missing a step. "There! See! Sober'n you."

He shrugged his shoulders. "Well, what do you expect me to think when you start ringing in garbage collectors. Would you do that if you were sober?"

"I am sober. I showed you, didn't I? You want me to walk a straight line again?"

"No, never mind. Maybe I better kill you and search your pockets again."

"And maybe you better keep out of my pockets and get back to business. Where were we?"

Suddenly the room began to spin around, and a minor panic seized Jane. "Listen, John Joseph," she said. "I think maybe you are right. I am getting a little tight. So maybe you better go home now."

"Home? Why? I like it here!"

"Mr. Swazey, I can read your mind. You would like to see me get real drunk, wouldn't you? So you could pick my pockets—"

"Aw, gee, babe. Don't worry about me. I'm a very gentle guy. I won't hurt you."

"I'll say you won't. Because you're going home right now."

"Not me," said Swazey cheerfully.

Something would have to be done and quickly, Janie knew. She was holding herself together by sheer will power. "Now look, John Joseph. Please try to be a gentleman. I'm going to pass out any minute. You wouldn't want to take advantage of a helpless girl, would you?"

Swazey smiled wolfishly. "Just what Edna always used to say," he declared, verbally licking his chops.

Jane staggered to the table and took the bottle. There was very little in it now.

"That's the girl, pigeon," said Swazey. "Have another drink to our friendship." He had a silly grin on his face.

Jane lifted the bottle and brought it down with all her strength on the top of Swazey's unsuspecting head. She wished as she did it that it was a less dangerous weapon, but she had no choice. He said, "unhph," and a glazed look came into his eyes.

Jane dropped the bottle. "I've killed him!" she moaned. She shook Swazey's inert form and to her horror his body dropped off the chair and onto the floor, where it sprawled face down in a grotesque position.

Jane's face was colorless. "Johnny," she mumbled. "I've got to call Johnny." She stumbled toward her bedside phone, reached for it, and fell flat across the bed, out cold.

It was a bright and cheerful morning as Johnny, with a slightly worried look, gave Jane's bell the three short and one long buzz. He had hoped she would call for him, but when she hadn't he had gone around to her house.

His buzz brought no answer. He pushed again and waited impatiently. Still no answer.

He pushed a different bell and the door buzzed back immediately. He made his way in, and to the lady who was opening her door in response to the ring, he mumbled, "Sorry—I rang the wrong bell by mistake."

She looked at him suspiciously for a second, then slammed her door. Johnny went up the stairs, two at a time. At Jane's entrance he pushed her bell firmly and repeatedly. He could hear it ringing inside, but there was no answer.

He tried the door. To his surprise, it was unlocked. He went in.

The inert figure of a man sprawled face down on the floor greeted him. Johnny grew pale. He dashed into the other room. Jane's body across the bed was frighteningly still.

Johnny grabbed the phone, dialed the operator and shouted: "I want an ambulance!" He gave the address and hung up.

He turned his attention back to Jane. Her skin seemed chalky and her forehead was wet with perspiration.

He tried to sit her up, but as soon as he relaxed his support she flopped right back again. He turned her over to see if there was any sign of violence. There was no blood to be seen anywhere.

He sighed with relief. But it was short lived. "Poisoned!" he thought. "That's what it is. She was poisoned! Where is that ambulance?"

As though in answer to his call, he heard the clanging of the ambulance bell. He rushed down the stairs and called, "This way," to the doctor, then rushed up again, the man in white at his heels.

"What's this—what's this?" asked the doctor, surveying the figure on the floor.

"Never mind him," said Johnny. "In here." He was in the bedroom.

"Phew," the young doctor whistled. "Looks like some party."

"She was poisoned!" Johnny explained.

The doctor's eyebrows went up. He looked into Jane's eyes and into her throat. He dropped her back onto the bed and went into the living room where he gave the man's figure a cursory examination.

"Well? Well?" Johnny was demanding. "What is it?"

"So you think they were poisoned, huh?"

"Weren't they?"

"That's a good one. You guys don't care what you call out the ambulance for, do you?"

"But I don't understand—" Johnny was growing wilder and wilder in the face of the interne's indifference.

"I want to know what's the matter with this girl!" he shouted.

There was a noise from the other room. John Joseph Swazey was staggering to his feet. He came into the bedroom, holding his head. "What hit me?" he said. "We were talking when all of a sudden I don't remember anything. What happened?"

A light dawned on John Angel. "Are you Swazey?" he demanded.

"Uh-huh. But what happened? Who are you? And what's the matter with the babe?" He pointed to Jane.

Jane selected just that minute to flutter her eyelids and moan, "Johnny."

Swazey looked around wildly. "Hey, you white wing. You here with an ambulance?" he demanded of the interne.

"Yep."

"Then there'll be a cop along any minute. Lemme out of here!" and he dashed out of the door and down the stairs.

Johnny lifted his dazed look from Jane to the interne and back again. "What's going on here?" he demanded.

"That's what I want to know, too," came a new voice from the doorway. A policeman almost filled the frame. He had a notebook and pencil in his hand. "An accident?"

"Oh, my head!" moaned Jane.

"No," said the interne. "Just a couple of drunks. One scrammed. The other"—he pointed to Jane— "is just snapping out of it."

Johnny was furious. "Don't you call my girl 'just a drunk'," he shouted pugnaciously.

"Your girl, huh?"

"Yes, my girl!"

"Well, don't get sore at *me!* Put *her* on a leash."

"I am not drunk!" from the bed. "I can walk a straight line. I'll show you." She began to get up and noticed how disheveled her clothes were. "You gentlemen," she said acidly, "might at least have pulled my skirt down while you were arguing about me."

"It doesn't mean anything to me," said the interne. "I'm a doctor."

"That's not the story I get from the nurses," Jane snapped back.

She had managed to reach her feet and stood swaying, holding her head. "Butterflies," she commented. "They look so sweet and pretty, but when they get inside and start waving their wings—"

Johnny tried to be very commanding. He said, "Janie" in a very stern voice.

She looked up at him. "Oh, darling. I'm so glad to see you. I was trying to call you up when it happened."

"What happened?"

She thought for a moment, then shook her head hopelessly. "I don't know. I can't remember."

"Fine thing," he snorted. "I find Swazey up here and you don't remember what happened."

"Well, I wasn't the one who decided I should meet him. It was all part of the murder. But he was real nice."

"Hey, what's this about a murder?" demanded the cop.

"Oh, it's just a private murder," Jane brushed him off. "But you're a fine one to talk, Johnny Angel—you—you Mormon you. Get out of my apartment. I never want to see you again."

Janie was near tears at the memory of Johnny entering Mae Wells' apartment. He was completely nonplussed.

He opened his mouth, but could find no answer.

Janie looked at her watch. "My goodness! Look at the time. I'll be late to work again!" and she dashed for the bathroom.

The three men just looked at each other.

Finally the cop said: "Look here, young feller—there ain't no such thing as a private murder. You better tell me what she was talking about."

"Oh, that," said Johnny.

"Yes, that!"

"Hallucinations," said Johnny. "Imagining things. She must have dreamed it up while she was drunk."

"She was drunk enough," said the interne.

Johnny gave him a dirty look.

Jane skimmed out of the bathroom. "Would you gentlemen please get out of here so that I can change my dress!" It wasn't a question. It was a command.

The three of them drifted into the living room.

In a moment, Jane darted out headed for the front door. The pallor of her face was hidden by some hastily but skillfully applied make-up. She had on a fresh summery print dress. No one could possibly have guessed to look at her that ten minutes before she had been stretched out in an alcoholic stupor.

"Wait a minute there, miss," called the cop. "I've got to make a report on this. You'll have to answer some questions."

"That's what you think," said Jane. "I've got to get to my job or I won't have any."

"But my report—"

"Invent one." She was out of the door. As she flew down the stairs, she threw back to them, "No work, no eat. And I like to eat."

Johnny dove for the door and ran down after her, yelling, "Janie—wait, Janie."

She acted as though she didn't hear him.

The cop and the interne stood looking at each other.

The policeman threw up his hands in a gesture of despair. The interne nodded. "Nuts!" he said.

They left the apartment and walked ponderously down to the street.

CHAPTER 8

The rhythm of the machinery had a somewhat soothing effect on Johnny. His own machine had its own little song that went whisht-zurr—cul-lank! Whisht-zurr—cul-lank! over and over and over. Johnny knew the song so well that he could detect the most minute deviation in key and quickly make the adjustment necessary to return it to perfect balance.

A machine can grow on a man, especially a good machine, for what is a machine but an extension of a man's hands? After getting to know a machine a man will give it as much care and affection as he gives his own hands, for the machine has become a part of him.

All about him other machines sang their own songs in a hundred different keys and a hundred different melodies. They all blended into one. To the uninitiated this was just clatter and racket. To the machine-tenders it was a symphony of a hundred instruments, and there wasn't a man who wouldn't notice immediately if one of the instruments was blowing sour.

Johnny's machine, which he had affectionately dubbed Genevieve, had been used in the days before Hitler, to shape metal containers for Ladies' Luxurious Lipsticks. Now it consumed the same thin metal strips but spat out no lipstick holder, but an oddly bent and notched piece of metal, which when fitted into its proper place on a gun stock, would act as a safety catch and prevent the gun from discharging accidentally.

Every ten minutes he would stop his machine, pick up the tray into which the machine dropped the completed catches, and carry it across the building to the department where the catches were fitted on to the stocks. The trip there and back, picking up a new tray on the way, took five minutes.

It was that trip which burned Johnny up. "If," he said, "they would use unskilled labor to carry the trays, or better still, rig up a little conveyor belt to it, I'd never have to stop the machine. It could be going every minute of the day, instead of only ten out of each fifteen minutes. When we get the union plan in, all these things will be changed."

The same slipshod methods held true in many other divisions of work. It was the plan to correct these evils that the Union had presented to J. P. Hirdler.

Today, however, the music of the machines did not prevent Johnny's mind from wandering. He was definitely not happy. He didn't know whether he had a girl or not. He didn't know whether he wanted her if he had her. He wasn't narrow-minded, but his pride was sorely wounded.

All during the morning he ate himself up with jealousy. He had his lunch with Bill Lawrence as usual, and poured out his heart. Bill listened sympathetically, then said, "I think you're getting yourself upset about nothing, Johnny. After all, she didn't want to see Swazey. She was just doing her duty!"

"Yeah, but where does duty leave off and pleasure begin?"

"You're acting like a jealous kid. You'll find out you have nothing to worry about. Why don't you call her and make a date for tonight. She'll be feeling better and you'll get the whole thing straightened out."

"Maybe so," said John, "but I doubt it."

"It's worth trying. Meanwhile, getting back to murder, I saw Ethel."

"Find out anything?"

"Plenty." Lawrence lowered his voice. "She remembered Angell from my description. He came without an appointment and asked for old J.P. himself. Ethel told him he'd have to arrange an appointment first, but he insisted that she call in and say that Mr. Lindbergh wanted to see him."

"Lindbergh?"

"Yep. Obviously that's a password. It got him right in."

"So he was there to see the big shot himself!"

"Yes. And that's not all. Ethel particularly remembered because it was the first excitement she'd had in months. About ten minutes after he went in old J.P. started yelling. She couldn't make out the words, but she could tell he was yelling all right. Then Angell opened the door to come out and she heard J.P. shout, 'It's blackmail—that's what it is.' Angell closed the door and went away hopping mad. She didn't hear any more."

Johnny Angel's eyes were wide. "I wish," he said, "I knew just what it all meant."

"So do I," said Bill. "Time to be getting back to the bench. Coming?"

"I'm going to try my luck with Jane first," said Johnny and slid into a phone booth.

Jane's voice was crisp and cool when she answered him.

He stuttered all over himself, finally getting out the suggestion that they have a long talk that evening.

"I'm sorry, Mr. Angel," she said. "I'm otherwise engaged this evening. Mr. Hirdler is calling for me."

"But," Johnny started. He stopped as he recognized the click of her hang up.

His afternoon was more full of gall and wormwood than his morning had been. When he headed homeward at night, he directed his steps toward Jane's house. Otherwise engaged or not, he was going to have it out with her for once and for all.

Jane had spent quite the most miserable day of her existence. She had reached her office only two minutes before Mr. Riggs, but it had been at the cost of going breakfastless. Perhaps that was just as well, for at lunch time the butterflies were still active in her head and stomach and just the smell of food quickly drove her from the restaurant where she had gone to eat.

There was a leadenness about her fingers which slowed down her work considerably and each hour seemed endless.

When quitting time came she waited for Mr. Riggs to summon her with her book. She half hoped he would, so that she might see his expression when she hurled the book at his face, but fortunately for both Jane and Mr. Riggs he couldn't think of a single unnecessary letter to dictate.

When she reached the street she saw the long black low-slung car pulled up in front of the door. She recognized it immediately. J. P. Hirdler, Jr., was waving to her. She walked over.

"Hop in," he said smiling. "I'm the fairy prince calling for his princess."

"No prince was ever more welcome!" Jane's stomach had been revolting at the thought of the crowded subway ride home. She had even considered the extravagance of taking a cab. Of course, this was ever so much better. She hopped in with alacrity. "I didn't expect you here. You said, on the phone, that you'd pick me up at my house."

"I start my evening young and nurse it along," he said. "But the princess looks a little haggard this evening. Can we pop in somewhere for the drink that refreshes? Or will you have a home made one?" and Hirdy pulled out his rack of bottles.

"No. No. Not that," cried Jane.

"Oho! So it's a hangover. Well—I'm fully equipped for such emergencies." He fiddled around with several small bottles and handed her a glass. "Here, you drink this. It tightens up rubber legs. Come on, now. Drink it down."

Jane drank it and puckered her lips at its unpleasant taste. But within a few minutes her stomach stopped fluttering—at least it slowed down considerably.

"Well, how do you feel now?"

"Much better, thanks. What's in that concoction? It seems to have poured soothing oil on my troubled butterflies, if I make myself clear."

"Having had a few hangovers myself, you make yourself perfectly clear. It's a combination of clam and tomato juice with a little worcestershire sauce and a shot of tobasco to boot. The clam juice soothes your troubled innards and the tomato juice gives 'em a little nourishment."

"But why the worcestershire and tobasco?"

"For the butterflies. The worcestershire anesthetizes them and after they're unconscious the tobasco burns 'em up. Works fine every time."

"You should have it patented. It's certainly made me feel better. Why, I can even think of food now, without going green at the gills."

"Chalk up another success for Hirdy's Bring 'Em Back to Life Preparation. And where shall we eat? I've got the rest of the evening mapped out."

"You don't do things by halves, do you? Let's hear your program."

"Well, first we eat. Anywhere you say. Then we go uptown. A new play is opening tonight and I've got tickets. Then—"

"That means formal dress, doesn't it?"

"It does indeed. I'll shoot home and dress as soon as I get you to your house."

Jane's eyes were beginning to dance. "Go ahead—what next?"

"Then we make a round of the night spots and meet interesting people, and trip the light fantastic. How do you like it?"

"It's wonderful. You have no idea of how fed up a girl can get on R.K.O. and ice cream sodas."

"A girl like you," said Hirdy, "was born to wear evening clothes and be followed by long lines of admiring swains in tails."

Jane nodded vigorously. "I like wearing evening clothes," she said. "And going to first nights, and meeting interesting people, and dancing. I love it. It's life. It's living. It's exciting. That's what I can't make Johnny understand. He says it's all a hoax—especially the first nights and the interesting people."

"Hoax? He's trying to destroy your faith in the Good Life."

"Well, he says that people who make a practice of first nighting have to see an awful number of flops. By waiting for the reviews, you can pick the better plays."

"I must admit there's something in what he says. You do take chances."

"I don't care! I'm willing to see some poor plays. Don't you start siding with Johnny."

"By no means. And why are the interesting people hoaxes?"

"He says they're not interesting. The interesting ones are the ones who do things—not those who gad about the night spots."

"I say, that's not fair! A man can do things and still get out and enjoy life a bit."

"That's my argument. But Johnny says that people who float around places where the columnists and gossip writers can feed off their carcasses aren't the ones who do things. He says they're the publicity hounds—the pseudo-interesting people."

"We're at your house," said Hirdy, as the car stopped. "This Johnny of yours seems to have very positive ideas about things."

"He certainly has. But he's not my Johnny. I'm through with him. He's out of my life forever!"

"Swell." Hirdy grinned boyishly. "That leaves me a so much wider road, doesn't it?"

Jane wouldn't commit herself. "I'd better go up and make myself beautiful."

"Take your time. No hurry. I'll be back as soon as I get my harness on."

Jane went up and made her preparations in a leisurely manner. First she took a warm shower, followed by a cold one. That calmed the remnants of the loose feeling in her head. A good rub with a heavy turkish towel left her body tingling. The long sheer stockings and scanty underthings came next and then that gown she had been dying to wear.

True, she had bought it at Klein's for a mere $6.95, but it was a genuine Hattie Carnegie model and must have been made to sell for more than ten times that amount. For more than four months she had cherished it, waiting for the opportunity to wear it.

A few large red and white flowers stood out sharply against a sheer black background. The skirt was full and fell in dainty waves about her shoe tips. From waist to hips the fit was snug.

She looked at herself in the mirror. "Callipygian, all right," she said aloud.

She combed her hair up so that it resembled a golden halo about her head and applied her makeup judiciously.

One last look in the mirror. The dress was cut just low enough at the neck to expose the upper arched curves of the breasts, in a tantalizing manner. She was satisfied with her survey. She didn't realize how long she had been until she heard the bell. She looked at the clock. Almost an hour had elapsed. She went to the door.

Hirdy stood there, his stiff white shirt front glistening. There was genuine admiration in his eyes.

"Like?" she asked.

"Like isn't the word. Why, you're—excruciating. You'll kill 'em. Knock 'em dead. I knew you were beautiful, but I never suspected—"

Jane blushed prettily. "You're just being nice."

"Lord, no. You're ravishing. Come on, let's get out of here. I want to show you off to the world. It's a crime to keep you away from your public a minute more than is necessary."

"Ready in a minute."

"Want me to carry anything for you? Compact? Keys? Anything like that?"

"That would be nice. Especially since evening bags are made so tiny. Here," she rummaged through her pocketbook and handed him compact, lipstick, and keys, which he tucked into his pockets. She held up her change purse. "Should I take mad money?"

"What for? A fairy princess like you need only wish and your every desire will be granted."

"You'll have me believing you if you keep up that line."

"Why not? Let yourself go and believe you're gorgeous. Because you really are, you know."

"I wonder," said Jane, "what to do with these?" She had taken the original code messages from her pocketbook. "Should I leave them here?"

"What are they?"

She told him.

"Humm. The whole case may swing on them. I'd take them along if I were you. Here, I can tuck them into my inside pocket and they'll be safe."

"Thanks. That'll be a load off my mind."

Just as she was about to turn the papers over to Hirdy the bell jarred loudly. Jane went to the door, still holding the codes in her hand.

Johnny Angel walked into the room with a dogged look on his face. When he saw Jane he just stood drinking her in with his eyes. The dogged look changed to one of adulation.

"What can I do for you, Mr. Angel?" asked Jane, coolly.

"I, uh, well you see, I wanted to—gosh, Janie, you look beautiful!"

"Just look it, hey? Thank you, Mr. Angel. Good evening. We've got to be going now. Come on, Hirdy."

"Oh, so she really did have a date with you?" Johnny's tone was hostile. "Where do you think you're going with my girl?"

"Your girl? I'm not your girl and I never will be, Johnny Angel! So don't you start anything."

"First it's Swazey, now it's him. Can't I ever come up here without finding a man? Just what do you think—?"

J. P. Hirdler had advanced and took Johnny's shoulder. "Now hold on, Angel," he said. "Please remember you're addressing a lady."

Johnny pulled back. His fist was itching to tackle Hirdy's nose. A free for all would assuredly have started, had not the bell rung again.

This time it was John Joseph Swazey who came in and gaped. "Oh, babe," he cried. "What a get-up. That really is the nuts!"

He looked around. "What is this, a convention?" he demanded.

"How do you do, Mr. Swazey. This is Mr. Hirdler and that's John Angel. Mr. Angel is just leaving."

"Like heck I am," said Johnny flatly. "I want to talk to you, Swazey."

"Well, talk fast. What are you doing with my girl? And why don't you drift when she tells you to?"

"Your girl? *Your girl?*" Johnny was hopping with fury. "Why, you big overgrown lug, she's my girl. What I want to know is what were you doing here last night? That's what I want to know."

"Oh, I get it." Swazey felt magnanimous. "You're the guy that's getting the gate. Don't take it hard, brother. Those things will happen. Why, Edna and me were going along fine when that little cake eater moved in on me. That's how it goes, see? He moves in on me; I move in on you. You'll get over it."

Jane had gone to the bathroom, hopped on the chair and brought down the duplicate code notes. She pressed one set into Swazey's hand.

"Here, John Joseph. You take these. And no matter what else you think of me later you'll have to admit I did you a favor. I could have turned them over to MacWilliams."

"What are they, babe?"

"Mr. Angel will explain them to you. As for you, Mr. Angel, here— you take the originals." She gave him the ones she had taken from her bag. "And that finishes us up for good. Take them and solve your

own murders. I've got places to go. Come on, Hirdy," and she tripped
down the stairs with J. P. Jr. right behind her.

Johnny and Swazey stared at each other.

"I wish someone would tell me what this is all about," said Swazey.

Johnny started to leave without answering.

Swazey said, "Wait. She said you would explain these papers.
What are they?"

"They are the code messages that Angell was killed for!"

"Angell?" a light dawned. "And your name is Angel. The same one
that lived above Angell? I get it. And the babe? Don't tell me she's the
one was pulled in with you—the one they got classed as your gal?"

Johnny nodded glumly. "That's her."

"Well, the dirty, double-crossing—"

"That'll do, Swazey. Now come clean. What happened here last
night?"

"She bopped me. That's what happened. I couldn't figure it out
until I got home. Then I discovered that I got a bump as big as a
duck's egg on my noggin. That don't come from the liquor. Last thing
I remember she was standing near me picking up the bottle. After
that I don't remember. Say, who's the fancy pants she left with?"

"The new flame. He's got what she wants."

"So have I!"

"No. You got her wrong. What she wants is satin sheets."

"Well I'll be— I read about dames like that. Satin sheets, huh?"

"You're wrong again. But what's the difference."

"Big difference. No dame can walk out on me like that."

"From what you said before it's no novelty to you. You mentioned
something about an Edna."

"Yeah." Swazey's face fell. "Gosh. I wonder if I got B.O. or something."

"Well, it looks as though we're in the same boat. What do you say
we go have a drink on it?"

"Might as well. The best way to forget trouble is to drown it."

They went over to the White Horse Tavern and drank the first
four beers in dismal silence. Only then was the weight that Jane had
left on them lightened.

"Say," said Swazey, "what about these codes? Been able to figger
them out?"

Johnny shook his head. "No, but I'll bet they're important. It'll be a feather in your cap to have found them."

"Yeah, in a way. But it'll make MacWilliams a little bit sore that he didn't find them himself. You gotta be careful with a guy like that. Mustn't step on his toes. Now, if I could only figure them out—"

"I've tried. No luck."

"How about giving each number a letter?"

"There aren't enough numbers—only from 1 to 9."

"Maybe you got to add pairs of them together. Try that?" Swazey was examining the code messages.

"Yep, no luck."

"Did you try adding every second number?"

"Yep—and every third and every fourth and fifth. And backwards. None of them work. You got to find the key."

Swazey was scratching his head. "There should have been one in his place then. And I'll swear there wasn't. I searched it myself."

"You did a fine job. Most of these messages were found there after you had searched."

"Hey? When was that?" Johnny told him. "Well, I'll be a sonavagun. So that's what she was doing in the bathroom. And I thought—say, she's some smart dame."

"You're telling me! Waiter—another pair of beers." And having returned to the subject of Jane, Swazey and Johnny swapped stories concerning the relative merits of Jane versus Edna, until both were almost weeping in their beers.

Before they parted, Johnny slapped Swazey on the back. "This would be a better world," he said, "if there were more human cops like you and less like MacWilliams."

"Aw—most of the boys are all right," said Swazey. "It's the punks like Mac that give the whole force a bad name."

"You ought to clean them out. That's what you ought to do—clean them out."

"Maybe we will, some day," Swazey agreed. "Maybe we will."

Jane was in seventh heaven. They had had dinner at a quaint little place on 23rd Street called the Nautilus, and for the first time in her life Jane realized that fish and its accessories can be made into the most delicious, taste-titillating type of food.

The play was beautifully done, enthusiastically received, despite the fact that the author had sort of half suggested that Fascist killers were human beings after all, and might be beaten if they were only snubbed hard enough. She had enjoyed every moment of it. The admiring glances thrown in her direction by many men during the intermissions had added to her enjoyment.

The long low-slung black car had seemed like Cinderella's magic coach as it transported them from one night spot to another. A drink at the Stork, a couple at Twenty-One, a bite at Toots Shor's, a few minutes watching part of the floor show at Leon and Eddies, with Hirdy being received at each place as though he owned it.

"Just yell out if you see anyone you want to be introduced to," he told her. "I've wasted my youth getting to know practically all of the important people."

"But none of them look like celebrities," she complained. "They all look—well—plain."

"It's the evening clothes men wear," said Hirdy. "It makes us all look as though we came out of the same mold." His eye scanned the place. "Well, there's Buzzy. He's always lots of fun."

"Who is Buzzy?"

"Burgess Taylor."

"Oohh—I've been mad about him since I was sixteen. He was the star in the first play I ever saw."

"He's coming over. Like to meet him? The critics all say his last picture is the best thing Hollywood's ever turned out."

She was so excited she could only nod.

When the slight, handsome young actor passed near their table, Hirdy hailed him. One look at Jane and he sat down at their table and stayed for fifteen minutes chatting amiably and cleverly. Jane was so overawed she stuttered when she tried to speak. When Taylor left, she just sat and glowed.

"Want to meet any others?"

"I don't know if I can stand it. The girls in my office aren't going to believe me when I tell them that he actually sat and talked to me."

"You know, you could come here often if you just say the word."

She had been drinking champagne cocktails and she felt as though she could fly if she wanted to. She gave a great sigh of satisfaction. "It certainly is something to look forward to, isn't it? But now point out some more celebrities."

"Well—see the heavyset man over in the corner? That's J. Edgar Hoover."

"The G-Man?"

"Yes."

"What's he doing here?"

"All in the line of duty. He's keeping his eyes open for vice, I guess."

Jane gave a little shudder.

"What's the matter?" asked Hirdy. "Don't you feel well?"

"No—I mean yes. I mean I feel all right, but he reminded me of the murder."

"Oh."

"I wish it could be solved. It's like—like the Sword of Damocles hanging over your head."

"The police will get the men, sooner or later."

"I don't know. I'm not sure those gunmen did it. I found out something."

"What?"

She lowered her voice to a half whisper. "Those people lied when they said they weren't home at the time of the killing. Both the lady upstairs, Mrs. Anderson, and Ponds, the landlord. I don't think Mrs. Anderson had anything to do with it. She wouldn't have told me about it if she was guilty, would she? But I'm suspicious of that Mr. Ponds. I'll bet—"

"Oh, now you're romancing. He probably had a pretty good reason for saying he wasn't there."

"Maybe. But I wish I could find out."

"Forget it. Let's enjoy ourselves."

"You know what I'd like to do?" she asked.

"Sure—try another night club."

"No. I'd like to investigate Ponds."

"You'll get over it. You'll have forgotten all about it by morning."

"No—I mean it. I feel like superman. I could solve this murder just like that, I bet." She snapped her fingers to show how rapidly she could do it. "I want to go over to Ponds'."

"Forget it, Janie. It's just the champagne. It always makes you feel like a superman."

"Please, Hirdy, humor me. It's been such a wonderful evening. Let's finish it off by solving the murder. That would make it perfect."

"But the whole police department is working on it. Surely you don't expect—"

"I do! I don't trust MacWilliams. He's not trying to solve the case. He's trying to pin it onto Johnny. Swazey told me so."

"All the more reason for keeping out of it. If Angel is involved, it'll—"

"Angel isn't involved!" she snapped impatiently. "No more than you are. You were both at my house at the time. And I want to find out where Ponds fits in. Won't you please take me there?"

Hirdy tried to play the part of the dominant male. "No," he said flatly. "I won't. I don't want you to go there. At least not at this hour of the night. This is the time for dancing, not detecting."

"All right, Hirdy. Thanks for a wonderful evening." She rose and headed for the checkroom.

He followed. "Where are you going?"

"To Ponds. If you won't take me, I'll have to do it myself."

Apparently the dominant male act wasn't very successful. Hirdy assumed a hurt look. "Of course," he said. "if you're as determined as all that, I'll take you. I thought it was just a passing fancy."

When they sat back in the long low car, Hirdy lowered the window which isolated the chauffeur. The car was already weaving its way through traffic. "Which one next, sir?" the chauffeur asked, looking back.

"Take us to Charles Street near Seventh Avenue." The chauffeur turned full around, a look of mingled doubt and surprise on his face. "Did you say Charles and Seventh, sir?"

"So you're against me, too!" said Jane, a little petulantly.

"Oh, no, miss. I just wanted to be sure—"

"You heard right, Hans. I said Seventh and Charles."

The chauffeur turned back to his driving and headed south on Eighth Avenue.

Hirdy pressed the button and the window purred upward, giving the rear compartment privacy.

Jane nodded toward the driver and said: "Why he's—"

"German," finished Hirdy. "Hadn't you noticed it before?"

"No. Isn't it—well—a little dangerous? He looks so—well—menacing. In a Peter Lorre way. I mean—"

"He's been with the family since he escaped from Germany. Perfectly reliable. As patriotic as can be. When they were rounding up the enemy aliens, we gave our personal guarantee for him. So you've been enjoying your evening?"

"Oh yes! Thanks to you. You must think me a beast for breaking it up to look for a murderer."

"Not at all. I'm the beastly one for even arguing the point."

She leaned over and gave him a quick impulsive kiss on the cheek. "Hirdy—you're sweet! You always do and say the right thing at the right time. You *are* a little like a fairy prince."

"Well—I'd like the job of making your wishes come true—on a—shall we say—permanent basis."

"Hirdy! I do believe you're proposing to me!"

"Does sound rather like it, doesn't it?"

"But you only know me a few—why this is just the second time—Hirdy, I don't believe it. You're fooling!"

He took her hand and looked deeply into her eyes. "How long do you think it takes for a man to know he's madly in love?"

"Yes, but—really—this is too sudden. I know I sound silly. I always giggle when the heroine says, 'This is so sudden,' but I can understand it now because this *is* so sudden. What else can I say?"

"You can say yes. You don't find me intolerable, do you?"

"Oh, no, far from it."

"Well, then—"

"But Hirdy. You don't marry a man just because you can tolerate him."

"It'd be fun. We could really go places and do things. No worrying about a beastly job or money. I'll buy you a closet full of satin sheets and all that goes with them."

Jane sighed. "It certainly sounds heavenly. But—"

He nodded gloomily. "The ever present but. I understand. It's Angel."

Jane started to deny it, but stopped before she spoke. Then, "I wonder if it is?" She sighed again.

She knew the right answer to that one.

They were both silent for a few minutes, each with their own personal thoughts. Jane snapped out of it first. "A penny is offered," she said.

"For what?"

"Your thoughts, of course."

"Oh, I was just thinking I'd like one more drink before tackling Ponds. All right with you?"

"It's the least I can do when you've been so sweet."

"Fine. I'll tell Hans."

They pulled up to Juliuses on Waverly place, just a block from their destination. "Wait for us, Hans. We'll be out soon."

"Yes, sir," said the chauffeur.

"We're just going to have one drink."

"Yes, sir."

They went in for their drink.

CHAPTER 9

When Johnny Angel arrived at his apartment he found a note had been stuck under his door. It said, "Have some important news for you. Ring my bell, no matter what time you get in." It was signed, "Mae."

He went down a flight and rang Mae's bell. He waited a few minutes, then Mae opened the door. "Oh, it's you. I thought you weren't coming, so I went to sleep. Come in." She snapped a dim light on. "Have a drink?"

"No, thanks. I've had so much beer my eyes are floating now."

He sat down and she pulled a chair over so that it was directly in front of him and dropped into it. It was impossible for him not to notice the lace work at the top of her nightgown, her opened negligee.

He got up and went over to her. He pulled the negligee around her so that it covered the front of her. Then he sat down again.

Mae hadn't moved. She submitted passively to the rearrangement of her gown, but she was smiling. "Sorry if it bothered you," she said.

"I want to be able to keep my mind on your news," he apologized.

"Well, I had a nice talk with Mr. Anderson. In fact, he slept right in that chair all night."

"Humph. Seems to be a habit. Mr. Swazey slept over at Jane's last night."

"Is that so? Well, well!"

"Nothing of the kind," he retorted hotly. "He passed out. In fact, she helped him pass out by the judicious use of a bottle."

"All right," Mae interrupted, "don't get sore."

Johnny threw up his hands in despair. "I'm not going to be sore," he said. "What's the news you got out of Anderson?"

"Something very interesting—about our worthy landlord." Mae repeated her talk with Anderson.

"Thanks," Johnny said through a dry throat, when she had finished. He began to get up.

"Must you go right away?" Mae asked insinuatingly.

He nodded. "Yeah, I'd better. I want to see if Ponds is in."

Mae rose and smiled, obviously amused at Johnny's discomfort. She held the door open for him and impulsively kissed Johnny on the back of the neck.

Johnny almost stumbled down the stairs.

He wondered what he would say when Ponds answered the door. You can't just call on your landlord after midnight without some reason. He was standing in the little areaway in front of the iron gate to Ponds ground floor apartment.

There was no answer to the ring. Johnny looked into the window which was on the street level. It was open half way. There was a light in the rear room. Someone must be there. He knocked on the window. No answer. He pushed on the window. It slid up invitingly. Johnny stepped into the room. "Ponds," he called. "Mr. Ponds." No one answered.

He walked back to the room where the light was on. It was a little kitchen. A door opened from it into the small yard behind the house.

Johnny scratched his head. "It would be a shame not to look around a little so long as I'm here. Keeper of the arms—I wonder if Anderson meant that literally?"

There were very few places in the apartment which could be used as hiding places and the search was very rapid and relatively simple. Guns take room, and aside from the closets, no other probable place presented itself. The closets' contents were obviously of an innocent nature. No packages under the bed. Nothing at all suspicious anywhere in the apartment.

"That doesn't mean anything," Johnny told himself. "The stuff might be out in the yard, or down the cellar."

He decided against the yard, since that would leave perishable merchandise at the mercy of the weather. He opened the door to the cellar. He searched for a light switch, but could find none. He did find a flashlight nestling on a little shelf on the side wall. He lit the flash and guided himself down the creaking steps in its little round puddle of light.

It seemed terribly dismal and damp in the cellar. He flashed the beam of light over toward the furnace, unused since the beginning of spring. He began to move in that direction, for his light had exposed an electric bulb hanging from the ceiling in front of the furnace.

There was a noise of something moving behind him, in the darkest part of the cellar. Johnny snapped out the light and dropped to the floor, waiting. He could hear his heart beating in the silence. It was so loud he was sure it could be heard clear up into the street. There was no further movement or sound. He began to wonder if he had really heard something, or if his imagination— He counted off ten heartbeats, then called in a loud whisper: "Is that you, Ponds?"

Johnny was cautious. He waited. It seemed that he heard quiet footsteps, directly above him. Then another movement from the back of the cellar.

Johnny, still down, began to pull himself slowly in the direction of the noise. He had gone only a few feet when he saw it. A pair of eyes glared at him. Johnny stopped as though hypnotized. The eyes were advancing toward him, on a level with his own. They were blazing.

Johnny closed his eyes tight and kept them that way for a few seconds. When he opened them the threatening, glaring eyes were not more than a few inches away. Johnny gripped the flashlight tightly. It wasn't much of a weapon, but it was better than nothing.

Something rough and at the same time gentle rubbed across his cheek. The menacing eyes blinked, and something at his ear said, "Meow."

Johnny cursed and flashed his light on. The big, black tomcat was purring contentedly, with no idea of the trepidation he had caused. Never in his life had Johnny Angel come closer to kicking a cat!

He resisted the impulse and went back to where the electric light hung and snapped it on. Not many places down here for hiding things. The furnace. Empty. A water heater; in use. A pile of coal. A few lockers in which tenants could store trunks.

The lockers were all open with the exception of one. This one had PRIVATE printed on it in homemade black paint letters. A padlock which seemed to have been bought in the five and dime was through the hasp on the door.

"Just like Ponds. Even for his own stuff he wouldn't buy a good lock."

Johnny scanned the open lockers and then concentrated on the padlocked one. He went over to the coal pile and brought back the shovel. One smack with its blade and the cheap and rusty lock lay on the floor.

Johnny opened the door. It creaked loudly. He went inside, using his flash to give more light. There was a large pile of something in the corner, covered by a paint stained tarpaulin. He pulled the cover aside and dropped it in a heap on the floor.

Then he stepped back and just looked. The guns were piled in military fashion. There must have been thirty of them. Johnny recognized them as the latest model, for they had the most modern safety catches—catches which he might have made himself. Near the guns stood some cases. Johnny explored. Automatics. Bullets. A few grenades. Sticks of dynamite! He emitted a low whistle. No need to look further.

He hastily threw the tarpaulin over the pile. Footsteps creaked their way down the stairs. Johnny's heart almost leaped out of his mouth. He dug his hand under the cover and brought it out clutching an automatic.

The footsteps had reached the bottom of the flight. It seemed that there was more than one set of them.

Then a voice said. "You see. I told you there was no one down here. He isn't home. You'll just have to give up the idea for tonight."

That voice was familiar to Johnny, but for a second he couldn't place it.

Someone was answering the speaker and recognition smote Johnny. He'd know Janie's voice anywhere, under any circumstances.

"Then why was the window open?" she was saying. "And the light in the kitchen lit, and the one down here?"

"And what are you doing down here at this hour with him?" Johnny added his question to hers, as he stepped out of the locker and confronted her.

"Johnny!" Her eyes widened. "The gun—what are you doing with the gun?"

Johnny looked at his hand. He was gripping the automatic. He threw it back into the locker. "Oh, that. I found it. But never mind that. I want to know what you're doing down here?"

"Johnny, darling, you're bleeding! All down your neck!" She rushed over to him, handkerchief out.

Johnny felt his neck vaguely. Blood? What blood? Jane was at him, almost sobbing in her fear for him. She wiped his neck tenderly with her tiny handkerchief.

She froze stiff—looking from the handkerchief to his neck. Then she repeated the operation. She wasn't sobbing any more. She threw the handkerchief down and gave Johnny's face a resounding slap.

Johnny stepped back. "Hey," he cried. "What's cooking here? You don't have to smack me just because I'm bleeding."

"You beast! You rat! You double-crosser! You keep away from me. I hate you!" she stormed.

Johnny made a beaten gesture. "I don't get it," he said. "I've heard of girls that fainted at the sight of blood. You're the first one I ever met who went into a tantrum."

"Blood? Who's bleeding?"

"I thought you said I was."

She picked up the handkerchief and thrust it under his nose. "Does that look like blood?" she demanded. "Blood indeed! It's lipstick. And you've got it all over you! And you've got the nerve to ask me what I'm doing. Why I—"

Johnny didn't wait to hear any more. In high dudgeon he tramped up the stairs and out of Ponds' apartment. He went through the open window and into the street. Hirdy's car was standing in front of the door. Johnny went over to it and lashed out with a resounding kick against the front tire.

Hans, the chauffeur, who had been semi-dozing, looked out in surprise. Johnny answered his look of interrogation by kicking again. "That one," he said viciously, "is for your boss."

Such animistic displays were too much for Hans. He just raised his eyebrows and shrugged his shoulders.

Johnny felt a little better after those kicks—but not very much. He wanted to think. This whole business was beginning to get more serious than even he had expected. He trudged up the stoop steps to the red door.

He heard a little click. A click as a key might make in a lock. It seemed to blend with a tiny squish coming from the door itself. At the same time he became aware of a burning pain in his left arm, up near the shoulder.

He dove through the door. And when he pulled off his coat, he saw that his shirt sleeve was bloodstained. He tried flexing his bicep and found that though it hurt a little, he could do it.

"At least no muscle has been cut, nor any important nerve. It's my luck that whoever is gunning for me is a bum shot. But this time I may have better luck than last. The car was downstairs, and the chauffeur may have seen who fired the shot."

He opened the door a hit and peeped out. No one on the street but two ladies walking way down near Greenwich. Avenue. He went down the stoop and over to the car. "Did you," he asked Hans, "see or hear anything funny?"

"Well, yes," answered Hans.

"What was it?"

"You!"

"Me?"

"Yes. You came out of the house, kicked this car twice, and then went upstairs. I thought it was very unusual."

"I don't mean that. I mean something that looked or sounded like a shot."

Hans' eyes popped. "A shot? Who is shooting who?"

"Aw—skip it. You're no help."

Johnny went up the stoop again—this time walking backwards, eyes raking the street. Nothing happened. He got behind the sanctuary of the red door, then started upstairs. As he passed Mae's door, he thought: "She's a good kid. She means well. But she sure got me in dutch with Janie. Getting lipstick on my neck that way."

In his own apartment he washed and dressed his arm. The bullet had skimmed along the surface, digging a shallow furrow. A bloody nuisance and burned like blazes, but not really serious, he decided.

Just the same, and he shuddered at the thought, that little click might just as well have carried with it quick death. Six inches to the right—it would have surely punctured a lung or, perhaps, even his heart.

The thought wasn't pleasant at all. In fact, it was definitely menacing.

And that cache in the cellar was even more menacing. Something would have to be done about that immediately. Call the police? Last time he'd done that he'd run afoul of MacWilliams.

He decided to call Isherman. He dialed the number and a moment later a sleep laden voice answered.

"Sorry to wake you, Sam. This is Johnny Angel. I've got to talk to you."

"What about, for God's sake, at this hour?"

"That murder! There's more to it than we thought. There's a cache of arms down the cellar, big enough to blow up half of New York. And Jane's down there with Hirdler—damn it!"

"What have they got to do with it?" The sleep had evaporated from Sam's voice. "Is it their cache?"

"No—they've been stepping out together. She thinks I double-crossed her so she's—"

"Hold on there," shouted Sam. "You didn't call me up at two in the morning to complain about your love life, did you? Stick to murder. The arms are what I want to know about."

"Well, they're there. Down cellar. That's all I know about them. Ponds wasn't home and I looked. Should we tell the police?"

"By all means. But better wait until I get there. I'll be over in a jiffy. Soon's I can get a pair of pants on."

"Good. And Sam—"

"Yes?"

"Be careful coming up my front stoop. Someone just took another shot at me."

"Well, I'll be— Listen! Don't you let anyone in until I get there. O.K.?"

"O.K. I'm waiting for you," said Johnny and hung up the phone. He felt much better. Nothing like sharing your worries.

Then he started to think about Jane, and he didn't feel better any more. Sam's admonition flashed through his mind. "He's right," he warned himself. "Stick to murder or you're a dead duck yourself."

But he kept right on thinking of Jane.

CHAPTER 10

After Johnny stomped out, Jane burst into tears. Hirdy was most considerate. He handed her a large masculine handkerchief and then stood aside, pretending not to notice.

When she gave signs of letting up, he said, "Well, that's that. We may as well get out of here. There's still time to take in some interesting places."

She took a few last little sniffs and answered, "No, I'm not going to allow that brute to spoil my plans. I'm looking for Mr. Ponds."

"But we've looked everywhere!"

"Not entirely. What about those cupboards? And the yard?"

"You certainly have a one track mind. All right. Let's peek in the cupboards, as you call them."

The lockers offered no Mr. Ponds. The tarpaulin covered pile that Johnny had examined passed by without a second look. Obviously Mr. Ponds wasn't under the cover. So Jane didn't even remove it.

"Only one more place," she said. "The garden. If he's not there, I'll give up."

They went up the termite eaten steps from the cellar and Jane picked up the flashlight which Johnny had left on the kitchen table.

She opened the door and looked out into the yard. "Mr. Ponds!" she called softly.

She dug the light into the dark silence. In the corner, it picked up the back end of a canvas deck chair. She kept the beam on the chair. "Hirdy, look," she whispered. "The chair bulges out at the back. It looks as though someone were sitting in it."

She directed the light lower, under the chair. A pair of feet was sharply outlined.

"He's fallen asleep in the garden," Jane whispered. She tiptoed over to the front of the chair, and threw the beam directly in Mr. Ponds' face.

Hirdler, who was following her, had barely time to catch her and prevent a serious fall, as she dropped to the ground in a dead faint.

He took the flashlight from Jane's hand and trained it on the landlord. He felt himself getting a little whirly-brained.

Ponds was sitting with his head nodding forward, his heavy double chin resting on his chest. His trouser pockets were turned inside out. He wore no coat. His hands were folded peacefully in his lap.

Protruding from under the roll of his double chin was the handle of a long kitchen knife. At the other side of the neck the point of the knife showed.

"The man who did that," said Hirdy shuddering, "should be a butcher by trade!"

"Oh," Jane moaned. "It's horrible. What happened to him?"

"Apparently someone knocked him unconscious and then slit his throat."

"And just tonight I had to go searching for him. Poor Mr. Ponds. I found him all right, didn't I? Come on, let's get out of here before I get sick."

Hirdy reached for the knife and began to remove it.

"What are you doing that for?" Hysteria lurked closely under the surface of Jane's voice.

"To turn it over to the police. But maybe I should leave it here. They'll get it soon enough."

Jane couldn't get through the window fast enough to satisfy herself. In the car, Hirdy poured a stiff drink for each of them. She gulped hers without protest.

"What do we do now?" she asked.

"We'll have to report it, of course."

"Of course. But—there's Johnny. What was Johnny doing there?" Hirdy didn't answer.

"It'll give MacWilliams another reason for picking on him," she went on.

Hirdy still remained silent.

Jane turned to him. "You don't think he did it, do you?" she demanded.

"I'm not thinking anything about it," he replied. "It's not our job to solve the murder, but to report it."

"It's ridiculous. Oh, I know he's a dirty double-crosser, but cutting a man's throat is something else again. He'd never do that. He might punch a man, but to cold-bloodedly— No—not Johnny."

"But, my dear, I never said Angel did it."

"I know. But that's what you're thinking. And so will MacWilliams."

"If he's innocent, you don't have to worry about that."

"There you go. 'If' he's innocent. There's no 'if' about it. He is innocent."

"Then why worry? I don't see what choice we've got, Jane. We have to report it sooner or later. And the sooner we do it the better chance the police will have."

"Well, yes. But we don't have to mention that Johnny was there, do we?"

"Wouldn't that be concealing evidence?"

She looked at him coolly. "And you," she said, "are the man who only a half hour ago was claiming to love me so madly."

"I do," he replied. "But that doesn't mean that I love Johnny Angel to the extent of lying for him."

"Neither do I," she flared. "I don't love him at all. But—oh, what's the use? Go ahead. Turn in the alarm. I can't stop you."

"May as well do it in person," said Hirdy, and to Hans he directed, "Take us to police headquarters."

Swazey was standing uneasily and a little unsteadily before his chief.

"What," barked MacWilliams, "are you doing here? You're on your day off. You're not due until tomorrow morning. Or are you so drunk that you don't know night from day?"

"Nothing like that, chief. I was on my way home and I got to thinking. I better turn them in right away, I think, because they're pretty important, and when the boss sees how conscientious I am maybe he'll give me time off for it another time, I think."

"You think. Well, why do you come in here and disturb me with your thinking? Why don't you do it at home, where no one will mind but the neighbors? Get your drooling face out of here. I'm not staying late for fun. I've got work to do."

Swazey turned sadly. "And I thought I was doing a good deed," he mumbled. MacWilliams was already engrossed in the papers on his desk.

When Swazey reached the door, he said, "Good night, chief. I'm sorry I bothered you. Who should I turn them over to in the morning?"

MacWilliams lifted his face. He was glaring. "Are you still here? Get out!" He looked as though he would throw the inkwell at his subordinate in another second.

Swazey slid hastily through the door. "I thought they might be decoded by morning if I turned them in now, that's all," he said as he slammed the door behind him.

Only one word of his mumble penetrated to MacWilliams. That word had something to do with codes. He jumped out of his seat and dashed from behind the desk to the door. A swift pull and he was in the corridor. Swazey had only gone five or six steps when he heard MacWilliams shouting. "Hey, you. Swazey!"

"I'm going, sir," said Swazey and hastened his walk.

"Come back here!"

Swazey retraced his steps a little timidly. "I didn't mean to offend you, sir," he said.

"No offense. Did I hear you say something about a code?"

"Yes, sir. That's what I was trying to tell you about. That's what I came down for, especially."

"Well, you're here now. Why don't you tell me? What are you babbling about?"

Swazey pulled the code messages out. "Here they are," he said.

"Yes, but *what* are they?"

"Why, the codes!"

"Which codes?"

"In the Angell case."

"That's what I wanted to know." MacWilliams grabbed them. "Good work, Swazey. Very good. I'll remember you for this."

Swazey beamed. He was about to ask for some time off, but MacWilliams asked, "How did you get them?"

"Well," lied John Joseph, "it's like this. I figured right from the start that that babe of Angel's knew more than she was saying, so I decided to keep my eye on her. I gave up my whole free day to get acquainted, just to see what I could find out."

"If I know you," MacWilliams said, "it wasn't her codes you were interested in."

"Aw chief." Swazey looked hurt. "You shouldn't say things like that. Well—anyway she had 'em. Both sets. And I got one."

"Both sets! Do you mean to say there was another set?"

"Sure. She made copies. She gave them to her boy friend—ex-boy friend now, I guess."

"You mean Angel?"

"Sure, Angel. He's a nice guy. We had a coupla beers together. He's got the other set but he can't figger them out."

"Angel—always Angel!" MacWilliams was storming back and forth in his office. "Everywhere I turn there's Angel." He swore vividly and long.

"But, chief, I don't understand," said Swazey. "What's the difference if Angel has the other set? We don't need more than one set to decode, do we?"

"Sure you don't understand. You don't understand anything!" MacWilliams' face was almost purple and he pointed to the door shouting, "Get out, you idiot—get out."

Swazey got out. He had been gone only a few minutes when there was a knock on MacWilliams' door. MacWilliams picked up the inkwell and called, "Come in." If this was that dumb Swazey again, he was surely going to let him have it. When he recognized Jane and young Hirdler he set the inkwell down carefully.

"Come in," he said. "What brings you down here at this hour?"

Hirdy and Jane looked at each other, wondering who should speak.

Finally Hirdy said, "We didn't expect you would still be here."

"Oh, so you think a cop's life is an easy one, hey? Well, it's not. There's work to do and when I have to go chasing around during the day the work has to be done at night. What's on your mind?"

"We've come to—uh—to—" Hirdy was uneasy. "Come to report a murder."

"Another one! My God! Who is it this time?"

"Mr. Ponds. The landlord of the house where Angell was killed!"

"All right." MacWilliams snapped into his professional efficiency. "Want to tell the story in your own words or should I ask you questions?"

"I'll tell what I know. Then you can ask questions to make sure I haven't left out anything."

"Good. Go ahead."

Hirdler told of Jane's desire to question Ponds—their ride down—the entry through the open window—search of the apartment, the cellar and the yard—and finally of the finding of the body.

Not once did he mention Johnny Angel.

Jane threw him a grateful little smile.

MacWilliams began his questioning. He turned to Jane first. "Why," he wanted to know, "did you think Ponds knew something about the first murder?"

"Because he lied about it. He said he wasn't home at the time and he was. Mrs. Anderson saw him."

"I see," MacWilliams said contemplatively. "You say the kitchen light was on when you went in?"

"Yes."

"And the cellar light, too?"

"Yes."

"The front window was wide open?"

"That's right."

"Humm. Sounds as though you surprised the murderer. He might have been hiding right on the premises all the while. Did you see anything that might be called suspicious?"

Hirdy and Jane looked at each other guiltily. Neither answered.

"Come, come now. You're holding something back. I can tell by your manner. What did you see? Or should I say, who did you see?"

"I'm sure," said Hirdy hastily, "he had nothing to do with the murder."

"Oh, so it was a who. Out with it now. Who was it?"

"John Angel. In the cellar."

The words sounded as though they had been torn from Hirdy most unwillingly.

"Angel!" MacWilliams bounced up as though a firecracker had gone off under him. "Angel!" His voice was gleeful. "In the cellar, hey!" He was rubbing his hands together. "Tell me all about it."

"But I'm sure he had nothing to do with it. The gun proves it."

"What gun?" MacWilliams was so caught by the very mention of a gun that he forgot to rub his hands for a moment.

"The gun he was holding. Don't you see? Ponds had his throat cut with a knife and Angel had a gun, not a knife. That proves he didn't do it, doesn't it?"

MacWilliams beamed. "Don't you worry about the proof, Mr. Hirdler. I'll worry about that. I'm going right up there now and have a look about." He dashed out of his office, wearing a broad smile.

When he had left Jane said, "I thought for a minute you were going to be a real friend."

"I tried," said Hirdy. "I didn't say a word about it until he asked."

"Yes, that's right. You didn't. But the second he asked, oh, boy, didn't you rush to spit it out! Even about the gun."

"But I thought that would show—"

"Yes, you did! That showed you up, Hirdy. You were anxious to implicate Johnny. Not very sporting of you."

"Now Janie, I assure you—"

"Save it. I'm assured. I want to go home. I feel almost as dead as Mr. Ponds. But if Johnny Angel is framed for that murder, I'll—" She left the sentence incomplete, and Hirdy feeling very uneasy.

CHAPTER 11

When the bell rang Johnny Angel went to the door and called, "That you, Sam?"

"It's me, MacWilliams. Open up."

"What do you want?"

"I want to talk to you."

"Come back tomorrow. I'm busy now."

"Open up, Angel, or I'll shoot the lock off."

"No! Not unless you tell me why."

"I want to talk to you about Ponds."

To Johnny that meant only one thing. The guns had been discovered. "How'd you find out about it?" he asked.

"Your girl told me. Open the door. No use trying to get away. I've got the house surrounded." MacWilliams lied. Far from having the house surrounded, he had even refused to allow his police chauffeur to come up with him, so anxious had he been to deal with John Angel alone.

"Why should I want to get away?" asked Johnny. He opened the door.

MacWilliams stepped into the foyer. He had his gun drawn. There was a murderous gleam in his eye, a harsh sneer on his lips.

"This is the end of the trail for you, wise guy," he snarled.

Now Johnny had known one humiliating experience in that little lobby with Whisper and the Runt. His face flushed every time he remembered that kick in the shins. Each time he thought of it he had told himself, "What a dope I was. I should have done thus and so," which is very easy to think of at your leisure and without a gun tickling your ribs. But—having thought out the whole plan of what he should have done in the past emergency, Johnny was automatically prepared for the present one.

"Put up your hands," MacWilliams was demanding.

How obliging of him. That fell right into Johnny's plan. He put his hands up—both of them. The left one, on the way up, pushed the light switch up, too, and the foyer was in darkness. The right one formed into a fist and landed on MacWilliams' jaw. Here MacWilliams made his big mistake. He had the gun—he could have used it. But when a powerful punch lands on a man's jaw and is accompanied by total darkness, his instincts are likely to be defensive instead of offensive. Unless he'd thought it all out beforehand as Johnny had. So far Johnny's plan was working fine.

MacWilliams pulled both hands up to protect his face. Johnny let go with his knee, catching the detective in the groin with the power of a mule. The detective bent double with agony. Johnny wondered what was holding him up. He uncorked a left and another right that was a haymaker. Both landed on MacWilliams' chin. MacWilliams didn't groan any more. His gun clattered to the floor. He thudded down after it. He filled the whole of the tiny foyer.

Johnny closed the door and snapped the light on. He looked down at MacWilliams and grinned. "Now if I can only get a chance to do that to the guy that's been shooting at me, I'll die happy," he said.

Then he calmly put his jacket on and with an assumed nonchalance, sauntered streetward. MacWilliams' big sedan was parked in front of the door, but the driver didn't even look up as Johnny came down the stoop.

He walked to Seventh Avenue and turned north. He had a queer feeling as he walked, as a mouse might have when cornered by a cat. "If the guys who've been taking pot shots at me don't get me, MacWilliams will. And he'll have the whole force after me five minutes after he wakes up. I've got to find a place to hide."

He racked his brains. He could go to a hotel—but that would make him too easy to find. He could take the tubes to Jersey City, but—well—running out of the state that way—no—he wanted to be near enough to be in touch with things.

He had it! The thing to do was to find a friend who would put him up for a few days. But where to find such a friend at this hour? The answer to that was fairly simple. Many village restaurants are all night affairs. He'd be sure to find one of the boys having a late snack.

The nearest place was Warnheims. But there he had no luck. Not a single person he knew was present. He dropped his unpunched check on the cashier's desk and left.

He cut east through the quiet dignity of Twelfth Street and went down Sixth Avenue. Only a few stragglers left at Harry's bar—none of whom he knew. Same thing at the Diner.

Johnny was getting a little frightened. MacWilliams must be up by this time and the cops might be on the lookout for him already.

As he left the Diner he met Larry Weiss. Larry was a lawyer who had given up the bar to join the army, and then when rejected for physical causes, had taken a job in a war production plant. It gave him the good feeling that he was doing something really important.

"Hello, Johnny. How's tricks?"

"Fine. Where is everybody?" Johnny knew there was no use asking Larry to put him up, for Larry lived very unprivately with a mother and two sisters.

"Guess most everyone's turned in—except the ones left at Raymond's."

"Thanks. I'll take a look-see."

He walked to Raymond's as quickly as he could without attracting attention to himself. He was in luck.

Gobbling up a tremendous dish of spaghetti marinara which would surely react on his ulcers the next day, and settling the problems of the world between gulps, sat little Joe Foster.

Foster was a journalist working on a national weekly. "Hi, Johnny!" Foster hailed and went right on with his argument.

Johnny sat down next to him. He spoke quietly. "Still got the penthouse, Joe?"

"Sure."

Johnny heaved a sigh of relief. This was manna from heaven. "Can you put me up for a little while?"

"Sure thing," Joe answered. He looked at Johnny questioningly. "What's the trouble—dispossessed?"

"No. I'll tell you about it later. Can we go right away?"

"What's the hurry? I'm not through with my spaghetti."

"It's very important, Joe, or I wouldn't ask. If I don't get up there very soon it may be too late."

"Gosh. You sure are being mysterious. But all right—if you say so. Let's go."

Outside Joe said, "Big enough hurry to take a cab?"

"No, let's not. The cabby might remember it if the cops ask him."

"Phew—so it's that way."

"Yeah—it's that way. Does it make any difference?"

"Only that we'd better get home fast."

They walked up Sixth Avenue. Once when a police two-seater turned into the avenue, Foster, spying it first, pushed Johnny into a doorway. He walked along by himself, whistling. The car cut across the street and stood waiting at a point where the riders could get a good look at him as he passed them.

Joe Foster flashed them a disarming smile and called, "Nice night, isn't it?"

All he got in return was a grunt. But the car moved on. When it had gone a sufficient distance, Johnny came out of his hallway and joined Foster.

"The way they gave me the once over, it looks like they've got the dragnet out for someone," said Joe.

"Yep—and the chances are it's me," replied Johnny Angel dolefully.

"In pretty deep, aren't you?"

Johnny nodded, and they walked along in silence until they reached Joe's house. No one, in looking at that building, would ever have suspected that it housed a residence. It had eight stories. The ground floor was used by a wholesale florist, as were all other stores in the immediate neighborhood.

The seven floors above it were lofts used by concerns that did fancy hemstitching, made ladies' silk underthings, novelty handbags and varied other nonessential commodities, which priorities hadn't yet caught up with.

Joe opened the front door with his key and locked it after them.

Johnny experienced a feeling of relief, and drew his first free breath since leaving MacWilliams on the floor. No getting away from it, it is no fun being hunted.

They began to climb the stairs, walking slowly. Elevators in loft buildings don't run after business hours. Finally they made the last flight and came out on a starlit roof.

A set of board slats led the way to a little building which had been erected in one corner of the roof. The outside was made of corrugated tin and was far from prepossessing. It resembled a watchman's shack on a construction job.

Joe opened the door, went in, and put the lights on. The lights showed a charming three room apartment. This was Joe's penthouse.

Johnny looked around.

"Where's Jimmy?" he asked.

Jimmy worked on the same magazine as Joe. He was the music and art critic. He and Joe shared the penthouse—probably the most ideal bachelor quarters in the city.

"His number came up."

"The army?"

"Yep. I go for my physical in a few days."

"Good for you."

Joe nodded contentedly. "Yep. Looks like I might get a crack at them. How do you stand?"

"They want me to stay on my job."

"I should think so," said Joe. "You're the guy that's making the guns we need."

"You sound just like the guy at the draft board," complained Johnny. He never had been fully convinced that it was just as important to make guns as to use them.

They sat looking at each other in silence for a few minutes, each becoming uneasy. Finally Johnny blurted, "I guess you want to know what this is all about?"

Joe shook his head from side to side violently. "No, I don't," he said very firmly. "I don't want to know a thing about it!"

"But, gosh, Joe. The cops are—"

Joe held his hand up. "All I know is a friend of mine is staying with me a few days. Just make yourself at home, Johnny. The dump is yours as long as you want it."

"Suppose you were to find you were hiding a fugitive from justice?"

"Bosh! I know my customers. If you're in any trouble I'll bet my eye teeth it's a frame up."

"Your teeth are safe, Joe, even if you make the bet!" and Johnny grasped Joe's hand and gripped it more tightly than he realized. "It's good to have friends," he said simply.

"The best way to lose friends is to go around breaking their fingers," said Joe, waving his crushed hand about.

"What we both need is sleep," he went on. "You can bunk in Jimmy's bed."

The penthouse had two main rooms, plus a kitchen and a bath. Joe and Jimmy had each had his own private room, furnished in his own taste.

Jimmy's room was lined with shelves on three sides and held a studio couch on the fourth. The shelves on one wall were filled with books—all sorts of books—but with those on music and art predominating.

The shelves on the other two walls stretched from floor to ceiling and had been specially constructed to size, for phonograph records, with which they were filled to overflowing.

Here, Johnny knew, was probably one of the finest collections of music in the city. Jimmy's love for Mozart had not blinded him to the virtues of Louis Armstrong, Bessie Smith, or the hundreds of other artists who had found newer and hotter forms of musical expression.

As Johnny undressed he thought of the many evenings he and Jane had spent at the penthouse with Jimmy playing new numbers for them and enthusiastically explaining, "Now listen for that trombone in the second chorus. It's not only giving variations—it's putting in a full-fledged spontaneous counterpoint."

Johnny sighed. Jimmy was gone from his records now. Doing a more important job. Fixing it so that we could all continue to enjoy music. All kinds of music—not just the Horst Wessel song.

Joe had retired to his own room. "Night, Joe," Johnny called and snapped out the lights.

Five minutes later he was in a heavy sleep. Its heaviness didn't prevent dreams. Dreams of himself racing around a furiously spinning giant phonograph disc, with MacWilliams in hot pursuit. Dreams of Jane coming to meet him, only to be stopped by Hirdy dressed in nothing but a satin sheet which sneered at him. Dreams of Ponds, using a set of stem-wound false teeth as ammunition for a tommy gun. Dreams of a hand that was tight in a fist, and ended in a stump just above the wrist, which kept poking MacWilliams in his nose, while he, Johnny, hid behind a bookshelf. Dreams of Jane holding out her arms to him. When he enfolded her he found himself embracing Swazey, and Jane had disappeared—all except her scornful laugh which lingered on. Dreams which verged dangerously onto nightmares and kept him tossing uncomfortably.

When he awoke the sun was pouring into the room. He looked at his watch on the chair near the bed. Twelve o'clock! He jumped up in a frenzy. Late for work. Way late! Then he remembered. No work for him today. MacWilliams undoubtedly had men at the H.A. plant waiting to drag him off to durance vile. Johnny had no intention of going to jail just to please MacWilliams. One taste of prison bars had been enough for him.

Under his watch he found a scribbled note from Joe. It said: "Here's a set of keys to let yourself in and out with. I told the elevator man that a friend is staying over, so he won't look at you too cockeyed. Coffee's on the stove—eggs in the refrigerator—canned stuff on the shelves. Help yourself. Don't read the paper until you've eaten."

Why that last? There was the newspaper folded neatly. Johnny reached for it—opened it. War news. Good and bad.

Johnny saw the item which occupied a lower right hand box on the front page. Its headline read, MURDERER K.O.'S POLICE—ESCAPES.

He felt as though he had been hit between the eyes with a hammer as his own name leaped out of the newsprint. Once over the first shock, he read the story from beginning to end. So that was why MacWilliams wanted him. Ponds had been killed! And by running away he had admitted his guilt. Or at least so the story said.

"The body was discovered by J. P. Hirdler, Jr., son of J. P. Hirdler, President of the H.A., and Miss Jane Allen," he read.

"That must have been after I left the house," Johnny thought. "Janie wouldn't have been so excited about that lipstick if she had just finished discovering a corpse."

Then the gruesome thought hit him. "What if Janie thinks I did its After all, I was in the house alone. I had the opportunity. I wonder—"

He wondered all through breakfast. The only thing that lightened his heavy thoughts was the newspaper account of the discovery of MacWilliams by his chauffeur.

"After waiting for fifteen minutes, Sergeant Clancy became suspicious and proceeded upstairs. He found Lieutenant MacWilliams sprawled on the floor. 'At first, 'said Clancy, 'I thought he was dead, but closer examination showed that he had been hit with terrific force by some large object'." Johnny looked proudly at his right fist.

"MacWilliams," the paper proceeded, "was rushed to St. Vincent's hospital, where after an X-ray examination, his condition was pronounced not serious. It is expected that he will be released today. Interviewed at the hospital, MacWilliams said, John Angel is one of the most dangerous murderers I have ever met. He should be handled the same way Dillinger was."

Johnny put the paper down thoughtfully. Dillinger! Dillinger found six men waiting for him when he came out of a movie one night. Before he could either surrender or pull a gun, they had pumped about five pounds of lead into his carcass.

That's what MacWilliams was asking for. A shoot on sight order!

Any possible thought of giving himself up was driven out of Johnny's mind. That's what MacWilliams wanted. They might shoot him as he walked in. Whew! Johnny's legs felt a little loose. The net was drawing closer. Right downstairs—out in the street, there were a few thousand cops and plainclothesmen—each with a gun—each hoping to use it on John Angel!

And besides them, there were the others—Whisper and the Runt, or whoever else it was who had beaten the cops to the idea of shooting him on sight.

"How," wailed Johnny, "did I ever get into this mess? All I want is to be let alone, to tend to my own business, and here, half of New York is looking for me with guns."

One thing was clear. It would not be safe to venture into the street. He would have to stick to the penthouse until things cleared up. But Janie. He would have to find out if Janie thought he was guilty. That couldn't wait. May as well know the worst right now.

He went to the phone and dialed her number. Before the ringing began he hung up hastily. "Ten to one," he told himself, "there's a cop there just waiting for my call so that he can trace it."

No—not only must he keep out of sight, but he must also keep off the phone. He looked sadly at the dial. At the other end of the wire sat Janie—waiting—wondering—worrying. At least he hoped so. It would be just too awful if she believed him guilty.

That's what he had to find out! He looked at the instrument longingly. "If," he thought, "there was only some way of talking to her in code so they wouldn't recognize my voice." It would be easy enough to tap out a message. After all—each letter in the alphabet was there on the dial and each group of three letters had a number. They were all there except q and you don't have to use q in a message. Only trouble was Janie wouldn't understand the code.

He pulled himself away from the phone. He must stop thinking about Jane. He forced his attention to a stack of new records. He put one on the player. It was a Duke Ellington number. He found its regular rhythm soothing—the improvised passages exciting. He tried the other side. Yes, music hath charms to sooth the savage breast—or is it beast? he wondered. The guy who wrote that knew his music. Like— what's his name—oh, yes—Orpheus. Orpheus and his lute made the breeze or the bees? or the trees, was it? bow their heads when he did play. Yeah—but *they* didn't have a double murder rap hanging over their heads. They could bow them—why not. MacWilliams and the whole New York police force wasn't after them.

He looked at another disc. Shep Fields doing a swing version of *Peter and the Wolf*. "Shep oughtn't to do that," he frowned. "Isn't it bad enough what they've done to Tchaikowsky, why do they have to start swinging Prokofieff? At least they ought to let the real music become known before they jazz it. Mixing classics and swing is like mixing two things that just don't fit together—like—well—like codes and telephones."

His head jerked up. "My God!" he said and stared into space for a moment.

He forgot all about the record that was playing. He jumped over to his coat, pulled out the code messages, and plopped himself in a chair at the telephone table.

"Maybe I'm all wrong—but it might be the answer." He examined the first code message—the one which had precipitated the whole thing.

There were those seemingly meaningless numbers running:

26682281631281662316719681273184 76844.

When he had last examined the code he had been puzzled by the fact that the highest number was nine. Obviously the numbers could not represent letters—there weren't enough of them. But if each number represented a choice of three letters as on a phone dial— well—that would be something. What strengthened his suspicion was the oft repeated single 1 at intervals which might well be the space between words, for on the phone dial the one was the only number which did not represent any letters.

He used a handy pencil and pad and drew up a chart that looked like this.

1 —	6 MNO
2 ABC	7 PRS
3 DEF	8 TUV
4 GHI	9 WXY
5 JKL	0 Z

Then he took his first word. 2-6-6-8-2-2-8 and tried to make sense out of it. He got some queer results, including ANOUBAT and BOOTCAT. On the fifth try he got CONTACT.

He was perspiring with excitement. Contact. A good word to be-gin a message with. Next 6-3. A choice of MNO and DEF. One of the letters had to be a vowel. That meant it had to be OD or OF. OF —con-tact OF—wait, there were more choices if the second letter was the vowel. That would leave ME or NE. M-E. "Contact me." That's it. No doubt of it. Next word 2-8. Assuming the two was the vowel, it must be A-T or A-V. No need to go any further. "Contact me at." Next word 6-6-2-3. Let's see. That 6-6 combination had appeared in the first word. Then it was the O-N in contact. Let's try that again. O-N-2-3. Only one answer to that—ONCE —"contact me at once—"

Time sped by. Johnny paid it no heed. He was completely wrapped up in his code. When it was finished he looked at the complete mes-sage. "Contact me at once or you are through."

"And Angell didn't contact him because he never received the message. I got it by mistake, and that mistake was his death warrant. No question that the one who sent this message is the one who is responsible for Angell's death."

He examined the other messages. They were much longer and more complicated, but he went to work with a will.

He found that as he worked the deciphering became simpler. His experience at cryptograms stood him in good stead. Instead of tackling the words in the order of their appearance, he took the two, three and four letter ones first. Then the larger ones took form with hardly a struggle.

"So simple!" he marveled. "And yet almost unsolvable without the key. And the beauty of it is that the key hits you right in the eye on every phone dial in the city. All Angell had to do was to take his messages to his phone and—but wait a minute. Did Angell have a phone in his apartment? I didn't notice any."

He shrugged his shoulders. No time to worry about details now. These messages were too interesting. Back to work on them. As the deciphering continued, Johnny became more and more excited. When he finished the second message, he spaced the words properly and added punctuation. Then he read what he had decoded.

Johnny re-read what he had written, aghast. "So," he muttered. "It's organized! The anti-Labor, anti-British, anti-Russian, anti-Semitic, anti-Negro, anti-American sons of bitches! And I thought it was accidental when one bird popped up in Oklahoma at the same time that the Big Wind from Texas started roaring and the sixth column press began yelping. But it's all planned and coordinated! What suckers we've been! Well, won't the F.B.I. love this!"

He set to work on the other two code messages. Here, again, instructions for disruption—for setting group against group. None of the messages bore a signature. The only clue to the sender lay in an appointment for a meeting, giving an address in Nutley, N. J.

"Some layout," thought Johnny. The enormity of the Ring was beginning to trickle into his mind. "Congressmen, Senators, industrialists, newspaper owners, columnists, commentators—phew—what has our side been doing—to let a gang like this run on unhampered? They're stronger right here than they were in Norway or Denmark! Yet Biddle piddles over guys like Harry Bridges, and let's these rats run loose."

A sound of the door creaking pulled him back to his surroundings. He looked around quickly for a place to hide, for he suddenly remembered that men with nervous guns were searching for him. He backed to the farthest end of the room. The door was opening, then Joe Foster's voice called, "Still here, Johnny?"

Johnny wilted. He sat down and wiped his head with his handkerchief. Then he called back, "In here, Joe."

Joe came in. He had packages in his arms. He nodded self-satisfiedly, as though he had won a bet. "I figured you'd hug the house after seeing what the morning papers said. Here are the evening ones—even worse. I brought in a stock of grub."

"Joe." Johnny grabbed his arm. "Look, Joe. I've discovered something very important. You've got to help me. Not for me only. The whole country is involved in this."

Joe looked at him, wide-eyed. "Sure I'll help you, Johnny. What do you want me to do?"

"Go over to Sam Isherman's house and bring him back here with you. He lives at—"

"I know where he lives. I'll go right after we eat. Come on, I'm starving."

"No, Joe. Before we eat. It can't wait a minute."

"Gosh—can't we call him up?"

"No—the wires might be tapped. And make sure that when you bring him back nobody tails you. They know he's my lawyer, so they might be watching him."

Foster nodded.

"And Joe—not a word to anyone else but Sam. This is much more important than whether they get me or not."

"O.K., Johnny. But I wish you'd arrange things in the future so that they don't come on an empty stomach."

"Greater love than this hath no man," quoted Johnny, "that he give up his meals for his friend."

Joe grinned and was on his way.

From the moment he left, Johnny's impatience rose. He kept watching the door, listening for every little sound that would tell he was back. He cursed the long drawn minutes as they passed. Time— time was so vital! While he waited there so helplessly these "Bogus Patriots and Noisy Traitors" were writing new editorials, more vicious speeches, to feed to millions and millions of unsuspecting Americans.

He tried to read the papers Joe had brought home. Joe had said the stories were worse. They were.

The arms in the cellar had been discovered. Some of the guns were made in the H.A. plant. Johnny worked in the H.A. plant—ergo—Johnny knew about and was responsible for the guns. Johnny was a union leader, the papers pointed out, insinuating that the union was probably involved in some plot to use the guns.

Johnny threw the paper down in disgust. "They'll eat those words," he promised himself. For want of something else to do while waiting he opened some canned stuff and ate it without appetite.

The minutes dragged into hours. It had grown quite dark. He turned on the lights and tried to read but was unable to sit still long enough.

He played some records, but found no pleasure in them. He talked to himself as he walked around and around.

The clock said nine thirty when he heard the roof door creak and footsteps approach.

CHAPTER 12

"He wasn't home," Joe explained. "I had to wait for him. Can I eat now?"

Sam Isherman said, "I expected to hear from you earlier, Johnny. Things look pretty black."

Johnny nodded. "I know. I read the papers. What does Janie think?"

"She's pretty well knocked out by it all."

"But does she think I did it?"

Sam shook his head. "She says you're not the type. But it's plain to see she's not very happy. What's your big news?"

"First, let me tell you this. Last night when I left Ponds' apartment, someone took a shot at me again. The bullet is in the red door. I'll bet that if we get it we'll find it came from the gun that killed Angell!"

"It's certainly worth looking into. I'll attend to it."

"And now," said Johnny, "comes the big news. I've deciphered the codes. Here they are." He thrust the messages at Sam.

As Sam read he began to grow pale. "Why this is—it's tremendous, Johnny. I don't wonder they were willing to kill you to get them back. 'Why it—it involves some of our biggest national figures in a fifth column ring!"

Johnny nodded. "Yep—but what do we do about it?"

"First thing we do is to make sure you haven't made a mistake. Let's see how the code works. What's the key?"

Johnny told him.

Sam worked on the codes on the phone dial for almost a half hour, while Johnny was consumed with impatience.

Finally the attorney said: "You're right, Johnny. The key fits and your translations are perfect."

"I could have told you that a half hour ago. What are we going to do about it?"

Joe Foster sat back drinking milk and munching sandwiches, goggle-eyed with excitement. He said, "What does it all mean as far as Ponds' murder is concerned? Does it give you an out, Johnny?"

"Gosh, I never thought of that! What do you think, Sam?"

"That's better, Johnny. Calm down while we figure this out. Then we'll decide what action to take on it. One thing is sure. Angell was a contact man for a Nazi spy and propaganda ring. It looks as though your boss, J. P. Hirdler, was one of his contacts. That explains, incidentally, why J. P. wouldn't put through the union plan for increased production. Also why Angell was visiting the plant."

"Well—Angell seemed to have stepped out of line. He was warned to get back or else. You got his warning by mistake. Before the mistake was recognized he was killed for it. So far it's pretty clear."

"But why was his hand cut off?"

"I don't know—yet. Let's go on. Ponds was probably in the ring, too. His job was to store the guns and explosives in his territory against the time when they'd be wanted. Perhaps he did the killing of Angell, too. You became suspicious of him. Apparently Jane and young Hirdler did, too. It looked as though he was going to be involved in Angell's murder. Ponds talked a lot and his boss became afraid."

"So they chopped up his throat with a carving knife!"

"Exactly. Meanwhile they've been worrying about whether you have been able to decode the messages. So just to play safe they take a pop at you every time you heave into sight, hoping to get you out of the case. Incidentally, the one bright spot now is that they won't be trying to shoot you anymore."

"No? Why not?"

"It would remove you as the goat. As things stand today it's perfect for them. No one has thought of looking any further than John

Angel for the culprit. If you were killed it would start a search for the real murderer. They wouldn't want that."

"You're right," cried Johnny elatedly. "That's a load off my mind. It's no fun, I can tell you, not knowing when the next bullet's going to— Oh, I forgot." His elation vanished.

"What's wrong?"

He shrugged his shoulders. "What am I getting so happy about? So instead of having ten thousand cops and a couple of gunmen after my hide, there's only the ten thousand cops left. And I'm happy about it!" There was a look of disgust on his face.

Both Sam Isherman and Joe Foster laughed. "What I'd like to know," said Joe, "is who is the 'they' you keep talking about?"

"They," returned Sam, "are the whole ring of plotters—and their dupes, too, for that matter. 'They' are the people who are doing their best to mislead the poor fools who listen to their talk and read their papers. But what's more important than the 'they' at this moment is *exactly who* sent these code messages. Whoever it was is the heart of the ring. That's the one we have to close in on first."

"We've got an address in Nutley. We may be able to find out something there," offered Johnny.

"Not 'we'," said Sam. "That's a job for the F.B.I. These messages must go to them."

"No!" Johnny jumped up. "No. How do you know who'll get them? How do you know that the very guy you give the codes to won't be a member of the ring?"

"But, Johnny, we've got to trust somebody."

"Not I! I don't trust anybody until I know where they stand. When the F.B.I. start investigating Martin Dies and Hamilton Fish and the rest of that crew, then I'll know I can trust them—not before."

Sam Isherman sat thinking for a moment. Then: "Tell you what we can do, Johnny. We can have some photostatic copies of the codes and their translations made. We'll send one set to the F.B.I. and we can send copies to a couple of newspapers, too. That'll force some action and expose the ring at the same time."

Johnny thought a moment, then relented. "Yep—I guess that'll be safe. But how are you going to get the copies made at this time of night?"

"I know a fellow up on Thirtieth Street who is in the business. His plant is so busy on specification work he's open practically all night. I'll shoot right up there now."

Sam put the material in his pocket. "Here's the schedule," he said. "I'll get the photostats, deliver one to the F.B.I. office personally, and take the rest over to Postal Telegraph for delivery to the papers. Then I'll shoot right back here. Whole thing shouldn't take me more than an hour."

"Do something for me before you come back, will you, Sam?"

"Sure. What?"

"Step in to see Janie. Tell her I'm all right. I don't want her to worry. But if she's been fool enough to believe I had anything to do with the murders—well—even if she does—you set her straight, will you, Sam?"

Sam wiggled his finger at Johnny. "Can't you ever think of anything but Jane?" he demanded. "Here you've uncovered one of the dirtiest gangs of traitors in the history of our country and what are you worrying about? A girl!" he answered himself scornfully.

"It isn't just a girl, Sam. Honest. It's love. And it's awful bad."

"All right, you young fool. I was young myself once, so I know how you feel. Now you just stay put until I get back."

Johnny grinned sheepishly at Foster after Isherman had left. "I can't help it," he said. "I love her so much!"

"You don't have to tell me," said Joe. "I understand."

"You mean," Johnny asked shyly, "you've been in love?"

This was a new Foster, one he had never suspected. "Been in love? Of course—and regularly. On an average of twice a week."

"My mistake," said Johnny coldly. "But my love for 'Janie is different."

"Of course it is. They're all different. That's the wonderful part of it."

"You're impossible, Foster."

"That's a matter of opinion. But to stop all this nonsense for a minute, did I hear you say that Jane had had the copies of the codes?"

"Yes, she did for a while. Why?"

"Well, if they wanted to shoot you because you had them—why not her?"

"Joe!"

"She was suspicious of Ponds the same as you were, wasn't she?"

"Yes, but—" Johnny tried to keep the full significance of it from entering his mind.

"But what?" Joe demanded.

"They wouldn't. They daren't."

"They don't seem to have many scruples from what I've heard."

Johnny stared for a moment, then grabbed for the telephone and began to dial Jane's home number.

Foster came over and with a surprise push knocked the instrument out of Johnny's hand and cut off the circuit.

"But Joe, I've got to know if she's safe! I can't wait. I've got to know now."

"All right. Keep your shirt on. There are other phones besides this. I'll go down and call her and warn her to be careful. Though you might wait till Sam gets back. He's going to see her, you know."

"No, no. He won't be back for an hour. I'm scared to death. Let's not wait, Joe. Go and call now."

"O.K. But you keep away from that phone until I get back. Promise?"

"Promise. Go ahead! Hurry!"

Joe went. Not too happily, but he went. He had always tried to arrange his life so that he only had to climb those eight flights once a day. Of course, up to 6:30 while the elevator ran, it didn't matter how often he popped in. Even his spartan spirit rebelled at those one hundred and forty odd high stone steps. But—he went.

Jane had been pacing her apartment restlessly for the last two hours. Once the phone rang and she caught it up anxiously, but it was only a survey ascertain to what radio program she was listening to.

After she hung up she had some qualms. Perhaps she shouldn't have cut them off so sharply. How did she know it wasn't Johnny, using that method of contacting her. But it couldn't be—it had been a girl's voice. Not that Johnny couldn't get a girl to do his calling for him—he seemed to be able to get girls to do everything else for him. She recalled his rouge-tinted neck with anger.

"The double-crossing rat!" she thought. "I wish he would call."

There was a gentle tapping at her door. She flew to it—opened it wide. It was a John, but the wrong one. John Joseph Swazey, looking a bit sheepish, stood on the threshold.

Her disappointment showed clearly on her face. "Oh, it's you!"

"Yeah, babe, I just wanted to let you know I was here."

"Well, now that you've let me know, you can take yourself off. I'm not in the mood for wrestling."

"You got me wrong, babe. I'm on duty."

"Well, go do your duty elsewhere."

"Can't. I've been assigned to watch you."

"What for?"

"Search me. But those are Mac's orders. Maybe he figured your boy friend might show up here. But he won't. He's too smart for that. He's a real bright guy—and a nice one, too."

"Yes he is. Smart enough to get in some two-timing between corpses."

"Don't you believe it, babe. I had a few drinks with him last night, and all he could think about was you."

Jane was pleased, but wouldn't show it. "Like a man thinks of his mother when he's in trouble," she replied. "Isn't it a little unethical for you to think this cold-blooded murderer is such a nice guy—or are you just trying to pump me?"

"Naw—nothing like that. He's no killer and I know it just as well as you do. So does Mac, I bet. Though like I told you once before, that won't prevent Mac from trying to railroad him."

Jane sighed. She wanted someone to talk to so badly. "Gee, John Joseph, I wish I could believe you. You act like a normal human being in your right senses—but after all you are a cop and—"

"Aw, gee, babe. Don't hold that against me. There are plenty of good cops. We're not all grafters and phonies."

"Well—so long as you've been assigned to watch me, you may as well come inside and do it. No use standing out in the hall."

Swazey came in and sat down. "Babe," he said, "you are tops. Not many girls would let a guy in after—well—you know what I mean."

"So help me," Janie replied. "I forgot all about that when I invited you in."

"Tip me off, babe. How did you do it? Last thing I remember you were holding the bottle. Did you conk me with it?"

"To tell you the truth," said Jane, "I was so close to passing out myself I don't entirely remember. Incidentally, what do you think will happen to Johnny if they catch him?"

Swazey shrugged his shoulders. "Never can tell with a guy like Mac on the case. Angel better keep out of the way until something breaks."

"But where can he hide?"

"Dunno—but he's found a place, all right. The whole force hasn't been able to find him so far."

"Probably with some girl," she said bitterly.

"Why should you care about that?" Swazey asked. "I thought you were kind of dickering around with that stuffed shirt."

"What an expression! Dickering. I wasn't dickering with him any more than Johnny was with that red-head."

"Which red-head?"

"Mae Wells. The girl who lives on the floor under him."

"Humm—so they were friends, huh? You know what I'll bet? I'll bet that he's there right now. It would be a swell hide-out. Nobody would ever think of looking for him right in the same building he escaped from."

Jane put her hand to her mouth. "John Joseph Swazey—if—if he is over there, would you turn him in?"

Swazey screwed up his face. "Babe," he said, "my assignment is to watch you. If I run into him, I'll have to pull him in. After all—he's wanted and I'm a cop, like it or not. But—if I don't see him I can't take him, can I?"

"You are a right guy," said Jane gratefully. "Come on, let's pay a visit to Mae's."

They walked over rapidly and silently. When they reached Mae's door, Swazey said: "Go ahead. Knock. I'll wait out here."

When Mae came to the door and Swazey saw her he gasped audibly.

Mae recognized Jane immediately. She said lazily, "Oh, hello. Who's your new friend? He's nice." And she looked Swazey over from head to foot from beneath half lowered eyelids.

John Joseph panted a little, but all he could say at this pulchritudinous vision was "Gosh."

"You sure know how to make them drool," snapped Jane in disgust. "May I come in for a minute?"

"Of course, dearie. Come right ahead. Bring your friend, too."

"He'll wait outside!" said Jane shortly.

From the look on Swazey's face it was plain to see that he regretted his agreement. But he kept it. He allowed the door to be slammed in his face and muttered, "I have to go to work on an iceberg and that beautiful, friendly babe has been here all the while. Shades of sweet Edna!"

Inside, for the first few minutes, the two girls acted like a couple of strange cats. Figuratively speaking, they circled each other, glared a little, spat a little.

Then Jane realized she was being foolish. She hadn't come to fight with Mae. She decided to put her cards on the table. "Have you—" she hesitated, "heard from Johnny?"

"No—what made you think I would?"

"Well, you were pretty friendly." Jane thought of the lipstick on Johnny's neck. "I thought that he might have come in here when he got away from MacWilliams. It was beginning to be like a second home to him," she couldn't help adding.

"No. He didn't. But look here, sister. If he had, he'd have been welcome. He's one swell guy. If you ask me—he's too good for you."

"I didn't ask you!" began Jane, but before she had finished she had broken into tears. "Oh, I'm so worried about him."

Mae came over and patted her on the shoulder. "There, there. Don't cry about it. You'll ruin your make-up. He'll be all right. And I didn't really mean it about him being too good for you. At least he doesn't think so. I tried to get my hooks into him, but he turned me down. So what are you crying about? I'm the one who ought to be crying."

Jane dabbed at her eyes and sniffed a little. "Were you—in love with him—too?" she asked.

"Well, I don't know as you would call it love—but it's the only kind I know. But it doesn't mean as much to me as it does to you. I've learned to bounce back. For instance, I could bounce right at that big husky you've got waiting outside the door for you. He looks like my class."

"Then why not have him in?" said Jane.

"Why not, indeed," said Mae and went to the door. A moment later she returned with Swazey.

Jane sat quietly on the side lines and watched Mae and John Joseph get acquainted. Neither one of them seemed to remember that Jane was there. The phone interrupted Mae's chit-chat. She excused herself and answered it. She spoke in a low voice and finished with an excited, "All right."

Instead of returning to her seat facing Swazey's, she headed for the bathroom. "Just going to put a dab of powder on," she called. "Come on, Jane, you can stand one, too."

Jane followed her. She closed the bathroom door and whispered, "Listen. That was someone calling for Johnny."

"Oh!" It was almost a shriek.

Mae put her hand over Jane's mouth. "Quiet, do you want Swazey to hear? He wants me to come to him."

"Why you? Why not me?" demanded Jane in a fierce whisper.

"You too, silly. They called you and you weren't home. I told them you were here. But Johnny needs help. I say let's both go."

"Yes. Yes. Where is he?"

"I don't know. A car is going to call in about ten minutes. He'll park downstairs and blow his horn three times. The man said you would recognize the car."

"How?"

"He just said you would. He didn't say how."

"What about Swazey?"

"We'll have to figure some way of getting rid of him for a while," said the practical Mae.

"He's supposed to be watching me. I don't want to get him into trouble."

"You worry about your Johnny. I'll worry about Mr. Swazey from now on. As for trouble—his type flourishes on it. Leave it to me. I know. But come on, let's get back before he becomes suspicious."

They rejoined Swazey and Jane marveled at the way Mae was able to continue her ogling and repartee without giving the slightest hint of her future plans.

For her part, Jane caught only half of what was being said, for she had one ear cocked for the auto horn. She got up and drifted over to the window and stood there looking down absently. Every time a car came up the street her heart would begin pounding, but they all went on, most of them turning into Seventh Avenue. One of them looked especially promising, pausing as it passed the house. It turned slowly into Seventh Avenue and stopped at the gas station at the corner. Jane practically stopped breathing as she watched the station attendant pump the limited amount of gas and accept payment and coupon for it. Then the car drove off.

Three sharp blasts of a horn sounded. Jane jumped. While she had been intent on the car at the gas station, another one had drawn up in front of the house. The three blasts! This was it.

She looked helplessly to Mae. Mae seemed not to have heard the horn, for she was deep in laughter over some *bon mot* of Swazey's.

Mae finished her laugh to the last pleasant trill and said: "Say, Swazey, I'm getting a little chilly. Be a good boy and go into the kitchen and bring back the bottle on top of the refrigerator. And some glasses. How about it?"

"Chilly? On a warm night like this? You must have malaria," laughed Swazey. "But who am I to argue about a drink." He got up and went into the kitchen.

Two minutes later when he started to come back with the bottle and glasses on a tray and a joke on his lips, he found himself locked in the kitchen. He set down the tray, forgot the joke and dashed his shoulder against the door. It was a flimsy lock and it took only four or five jolts to shatter it. He reached the window in time to see the car sweep into the downtown traffic on Seventh Avenue. He could see Mae's red and Jane's golden hair through the back glass.

Joe found Johnny biting his nails. "Well, did you get her?" the impatient one asked.

"No. She's not home. At least no one answered the phone."

"There! You see! Something's happened to her. I knew it. I'm getting out of here."

"Take it easy, Johnny. Just because she isn't home doesn't mean something's happened to her."

"I can't help it. I'm worried."

"Let's wait and find out if there's anything to be worried about. Here. I'll play you some music. Here's a new hot record release by Jimmie McPortland's Squirrels. Jimmy does a trumpet solo that'll knock your eye out. Listen!"

As soon as the record finished, Joe had another waiting. "Just listen to this one," he said. "See what Louis Armstrong's trumpet and Buck Washington's piano can do to 'Dear Old Southland'. It's a classic."

Record after record turned and gave out, and gradually Johnny's pacing became a little less frenzied. Just the same he kept looking at his watch. Finally he blurted: "Where's Sam? It's more than an hour and a half since he left. It's almost two hours."

The phone rang. Johnny rushed for it. Joe reached it first. "Hello," he said, then, "yes—yes—yes." He hung up. "That was Sam. He got the photostats around. They're all hopped up about it over at the F.B.I. He says—"

"To hell with that stuff. How about Jane?"

"Sam met Swazey. He pumped him a little. Swazey was assigned to watch Jane. Jane and Mae gave him the slip and rode off in a car."

"Whose car?"

"He didn't know for sure."

"Where's Swazey now?"

"Up at your house waiting for MacWilliams."

Johnny was out of the door and across the roof to the stair landing.

"Hey, wait," Joe shouted. "You can't do that. Sam says you should stay here." But Johnny was already halfway down the eight flights.

CHAPTER 13

Charles Street. Swazey. Johnny had to get there before MacWilliams. He knew that. He looked for a cruising cab. There was none in sight. No busses either.

A newspaper delivery truck was zooming down the avenue. It slowed down a little and the man standing in the back threw a bundle of papers toward a stationery store newsstand. Johnny ducked as the bundle whizzed by his head and hit the sidewalk with a quoosh—then slid up to the door where it would be picked up in the morning. The newspaper heaver grinned at Johnny. His truck began picking up speed again. Before it reached the corner, the lights turned red and the driver slammed on his brakes.

Johnny ran across to the truck. The paper thrower wasn't grinning any more. He looked a little frightened. He'd been playing a game of Scare the Pedestrian for a long time and now it looked as though it might be catching up to him. And from the determined look on Johnny's face as he ran, the results promised to be not very pleasant.

Johnny pulled himself up on the tailboard just as the lights changed and the truck jerked to a rapid getaway. He steadied himself, then stood erect. The paper thrower cowered a little inside the truck. "What are you sore about? I didn't hit you, did I?"

"Of course not," said Johnny. "Who said you did?"

"Then what did you chase me for? I can't help it if the bundle scared you. I gotta get it up to the door, don't I?" He had another bundle in his hand and he looked away from Johnny long enough to aim it and let it go at another newsstand.

Johnny looked out. Passing Fourteenth Street already. The truck was making better time than a cab. "All right, buddy," he said. "When do you hit the next red light?"

"Usually around Eighth Street. You mean you ain't sore at me?"

"Sure I'm sore. You almost knocked my head off. But I'll leave it to your conscience to punish you. Besides, we're almost at Eighth Street and that's where I get off. Thanks for the lift."

Then Johnny dropped to the ground, for the truck had stopped at Eighth Street. He hurried to cross the street when something whizzed between his legs, tripped him and brought him down in a heap. He picked himself up, disentangled himself from the bundle of papers and got to his feet in time to wave a fist at the fast receding truck.

"Well, the score is even," thought Johnny. "So now for Charles Street!"

He hadn't taken the first step when he noticed a cop approaching. He felt an almost overwhelming desire to turn and run, but he conquered it.

"You wanna make a charge against that guy?" asked the cop. "He threw them right at you purposely. I was watching him. I got his number."

"No," said Johnny. "It's just a game we play. He doesn't mean any harm by it."

The cop shrugged his shoulders. "O.K.," he said. Then Johnny hurried up Greenwich Avenue to Charles Street.

Pacing up and down in front of Johnny's house in evident agitation was the unmistakable figure of John Joseph Swazey. Johnny ran to him, slapped him on the back. "Which way did the car go, Swazey?" he demanded.

"Down Seventh Avenue," the detective answered automatically. Then he almost shouted. "Hey, it's you. We've been looking for you!"

"I know," said Johnny. "But never mind that now. Try to remember, Swazey. Isn't there anything you can remember that might help us to find them?"

"Nothing. Might have been heading anywhere down town—or maybe for the Holland Tunnel to New Jersey."

"Did you say New Jersey?"

"Yep. What about it?"

Johnny snapped his fingers. "It gives me an idea, that's all. New Jersey. Nutley! I'll bet that's it!"

A siren screamed. A car pulled up alongside of them. Johnny's back was toward the car. A voice he recognized as MacWilliams' boomed out. "I'll break you for this, Swazey," and the owner of the voice stepped out of the car which he had been driving himself.

No time for planning now. Only one thing was important—to get to Nutley. Johnny swung around. His left fist landed on MacWilliams' chin, his right on the lieutenant's jaw. MacWilliams stood swaying, like a man on a tight rope. Johnny didn't wait to see if he would fall or come out of it. He slid into the driver's seat so recently vacated by MacWilliams, pushed the clutch, stepped on the accelerator and shot into Seventh Avenue like a cannon ball.

There was a little cord near the wheel. Johnny pulled it. The car's siren filled the night. Traffic, which wasn't very heavy at that hour, made way for him. He kept his foot to the floor and the siren cord taut. He ignored lights, whether green or red. No one seemed to mind. The siren acted as a magic signal.

At Canal Street he swung west on two wheels and a minute's run brought him to the Holland Tunnel. He discarded the idea of slowing down to pay the toll. Perhaps cops go free, like on subways. Then it would draw suspicion to him if he tried to pay.

The car dove into the tunnel. Nobody tried to stop him.

MacWilliams didn't fall. Swazey helped to hold him up. Any honest referee, however, would have called it a technical knockout, for the lieutenant was hors de combat for more than the required ten seconds.

Swazey helped him to the stoop and sat him down. When the film left his eyes, he asked dazedly, "What happened? Wasn't that Angel?"

"Sure it was," said Swazey, then, seeing a way out of his own difficulty he added a little white lie. "I had my gun on him when you barged in and spoiled it."

"Where is he now?"

"He got away in your car."

"My car!" Then he repeated, two octaves higher, "My car! And you let him go!"

"I couldn't help it. My hands were full of you."

MacWilliam's was fully recovered and raging like a lion. "Not only gets away, but in my car. Which way did he go?"

"I dunno. He said something about Nutley."

"Nutley!" MacWilliams' excitement before was as nothing to what he displayed at the mention of that little New Jersey town. He pranced and raved like one demented.

To Swazey's mind, MacWilliams lacked not only control, but also dignity.

When he finally quieted the springs in his system and his voice, MacWilliams shouted, "What are you waiting for? Try those cars. One of them must be open." He pointed to a few cars parked for the night along the street, and made a mental note to see that everyone of them received parking tickets in the morning.

But the owners had unthoughtfully locked all their car doors with the exception of the battered old convertible whose top and right forward fender were missing. Its key rested invitingly in its lock.

"Probably got it insured and is hoping it gets stolen," muttered Swazey. When he started the motor, he could tell why. Asthma. What sounded like an incurable case.

He drove the car to where Mac was waiting and his superior officer climbed in alongside of him. "Can't you choke that wheeze?" demanded MacWilliams.

Swazey shook his head sadly.

"Well, never mind. So long as it runs. Let's go. Hit for the Holland Tunnel. And let's hope he's got gas in his tank."

At a top speed of twenty-five miles an hour they rattled downtown. After a bit of silence Swazey said: "We can never catch up to him at this speed. Hadn't we better put the information on the teletype?"

"And let them know my car's been stolen? Nothing doing. I'll get back the car and get Angel, too, before we report anything. Then nobody will have the laugh on me."

"Yeah. But how do we know where he's gone?"

"He said Nutley, didn't he? Then it's Nutley for us.

"But Nutley's a big town. I know. I once had a babe who lived there."

"Don't worry. We'll find him."

"But even if we do, we can't do anything about it. We got no authority to make an arrest outside of New York. Nutley's in New Jersey."

"Don't you worry about authority. This," and MacWilliams slapped his gun holster, "has authority anywhere. They'll thank us for getting Angel, no matter where we get him. Can't you go any faster?"

The car seemed to have slowed down. "Maybe," answered Swazey, "she'll pick up some speed when she gets her second wind. I got the gas button down as far as she'll go."

Which was a lie. But lies didn't seem to bother Swazey's conscience at all. Truth was he had no stomach for this chase and was hoping that he could delay it until Johnny finished his business in Nutley and made his getaway.

When the girls felt that their car had successfully avoided pursuit Jane called to the driver. "How far is it?" she asked.

"Just across the river," he answered.

She recognized the voice. "Why, you're—"

"Hans," he finished, turning back and smiling.

"Of course! And this is Mr. Hirdler's car. We rushed out of the house so fast I didn't get a good look at it. But I don't understand. How did you—why—?"

"It's very simple. Mr. Angel contacted Mr. Hirdler and Mr. Hirdler sent me for you."

"Oh, I see." But she didn't, entirely. Why should Johnny contact Hirdy, of all people. And why had they contacted Mae?

Jane knew nothing of northern New Jersey and the little house they pulled up to might just as well have been in Teaneck or South Orange, as far as she could tell.

It was a one-family house on a quiet little street, set off by itself. Apparently it was the only completed one in a whole development. Other houses stood silhouetted in the moonlight, but most of them had no roofs. It looked as though some giant hand had descended in the midst of the work and said, "Stop right here."

That is what had actually happened. The hand had been the one that fell at Pearl Harbor and the voice had said: "You will get the balance of your building material in time, but first we must use what we have for some much needed war factories."

Inside the one completed house, which had evidently been finished early so that it might be used as a model by which to sell the others, a light showed through Venetian blinds.

Hans was out of the car, leading them to the door. "Johnny is inside?" Jane asked.

Hans nodded. He opened the door. The girls went in. He followed.

Two men came to meet them. They did not surprise Mae, for she had never seen them before. Jane knew them and tried to scream, but Hans' hand came around her neck and covered her mouth. The Runt approached her menacingly, while Whisper covered Mae.

CHAPTER 14

Five minutes later each girl sat on a chair, hands tied behind her, a gag in her mouth. The Runt stood behind Jane's chair, Whisper behind Mae. Each man held a blackjack in his hand.

"Now please to understand me," said Hans gutturally. "I am willing to remove the gags if you will not scream. Not that it would do you any good. Nobody could hear you. But for safety's sake we would find it necessary to quiet you forcibly if you should feel the need to become noisy. Is it understood?"

They nodded and Hans walked over and removed the gags. Mae launched a kick at him which just missed, and he turned and with deliberation gave her a resounding slap on the cheek. "So now you can be comfortable, mine *leiber fraulein*," he said, "for a little while, anyway."

"I knew you couldn't be trusted as soon as I saw you," said Jane. "I told Hirdy so."

"Yes—and I overheard you, which is one of the reasons you are here."

"Where's Johnny?"

"That I do not know. But we are looking for him and if we do not find him soon the police surely will, which is also quite all right."

"What?" asked Mae, whose face showed the marks of Hans' slap. "What did you bring us here for? What do you intend to do with us?"

"That I cannot tell you at the moment. Sufficient that you shall not interfere further."

"They mean to—to kill us," Mae's voice quivered as she whispered to Jane.

Jane nodded. "Don't worry," she tried to soothe Mae, but found her own voice as unsteady as the red-head's. "You certainly cleared up things for me," she told Hans. "Now there's no mystery any more. You killed Angell and Ponds, didn't you?"

Hans bowed stiffly from the waist. "Thank you," he said. "You can see now why it was necessary to remove you from places where your voice could be heard? Such words as those spoken indiscreetly might bring the police to search for me with drawn guns instead of for Johnny Angel. I would not like that."

"Why didn't you just shoot us in New York? From what you did to Ponds, it's clear that you get quite a kick out of killing."

"Come, come, my dear Miss Allen. Surely you must understand that corpses cannot be strewn about indiscriminately without creating a furor. One, yes. Even two, when necessity demands. But four? No. That is too dangerous. Even your stupid police would become suspicious. Then we could not operate under their noses any longer."

"What do you operate in?" Jane asked.

"That is not your business."

"I know," Mae put in. "Anderson told me. Guns. Explosives. For fifth columnists."

"Aha." Hans' face was more menacing than Peter Lorre's. "I was correct to think you also knew too much. And thank you for telling me about Anderson, the poor fool. He shall not talk again."

"You're welcome," said Mae. "Knock all the Fronters off and see if I care."

Hans shrugged. "There are plenty more like Anderson. Some like these," he pointed to Whisper and the Runt, "must be paid to do our work, but the Andersons—ha—they are happy to do it for nothing. And one pair of Andersons can do us more good than a dozen gunmen. How they can set you Americans against each other. It is wonderful—no?"

"Yeah! Wonderful for your side."

Hans laughed. "That is the only side. You Americans have no side. You are too stupid. You keep yourselves busy hating and fighting each other. How can you find the time to fight us? We know how to do these things better. We organize hatred and make it work for us. Ah, he is coming."

The sound of a car could be plainly heard. Jane had heard it while Hans was speaking and hope had risen in her, but it faded with his last words. Evidently he was expecting someone. Instead of helping, this might bring closer whatever fate was in store for them.

Hans went to the door and pulled it open. A figure, seemingly all fists and feet, came hurtling in. One of the fists landed on Hans' nose, drawing blood and forcing him back.

"Johnny! It's Johnny!" shrieked Jane in delight, and Mae added her pleasure to the chorus. "Scream, Mae!" cried Jane. "They're too busy to watch us now."

They were busy indeed. There was a swirling mass of humanity in the middle of the room. It included Johnny, Whisper, the Runt and Hans. Johnny seemed to be pretty much the center of the vortex. His fists flashed like pistons. For a time he seemed to be having all the better of it and Mae forgot to scream long enough to shout, "Give it to 'em, big boy—for Uncle Sam. Let them have it," then she raised a piercing shriek again.

If anyone had lived within a half mile of the house the girls would have been heard, but Hans had not lied when he had told them they were isolated.

Johnny went down, but before they could tumble on him, he was up again. The Runt was stretched out flat, groaning. Johnny's size eleven shoe had landed in his solar plexus.

Hans, nose bleeding profusely, bent down and picked up the Runt's blackjack. Then he waited calmly until Johnny's back was turned to him, and brought it down with a clunk on Johnny's head.

Jane shuddered. Johnny stiffened, but stayed up. He turned his attention to Hans. Hans backed away, face paling. Whisper took advantage of the situation to use his sapper. It sounded like the cracking of a coconut when it landed and this time Johnny dropped.

Hans and Whisper looked at each other. "Phew—this one can fight—no?" said Hans.

"There are a hundred and thirty million like that," said Jane. "Your Fuehrer's going to find out about it pretty soon."

"Quiet!" stormed Hans. "Nobody but a fool would do this with the odds three to one!"

"A fool or a brave man. And we've got plenty of brave men—" Hans' hand smacked across her lips. Jane laughed. "Your men are brave, too, Hans. Smacking women. And being sure they're tied up first."

"Tie him up!" shouted Hans.

Whisper got to work. The Runt was still writhing. Soon Johnny was placed in a chair lined up with the two girls. His head hung at a grotesque angle. Jane was frightened for herself and scared for Johnny, but her predominant emotion was pride. Her man was a brave man! He had come through in the pinch. Even though he had lost, he had put up a good fight.

Hans said to Whisper: "Come inside. I wish to give you instructions. Bring your little Runt along." He looked scornfully at the hurt gunman.

Whisper led his buddy into the next room. At the door, Hans turned to the girls. "You will not shout. At the first noise I will personally silence you." He pounded the blackjack into the palm of his hand a few times. Then he closed the door after him.

The girls looked at each other. "Do you think they'll—" Mae couldn't finish it.

Jane nodded. "I think so. They couldn't afford to let us go now."

A moment later Mae said: "Let's not think about it. Let's talk of something else."

"What else?"

"I don't know. Nothing seems very important when you know you're going to—die soon."

"That," said Jane, "is what we're not going to think about. There's something I want to tell you, Mae."

"What?"

"I was very angry at you. I hated you. But I don't any more. It was just jealousy."

"That's a good one. Why, you've got everything from good looks to a fine guy. Why should you be jealous of me?"

"There's nothing wrong with your looks. And your figure is gorgeous."

"Oh, that," and Mae almost giggled.

"Look," said Jane. "Johnny moved. It looks as though he's coming to."

Coming to he was. After a few spasmodic jerks he got his head straight back on his shoulders again and opened his eyes. When he saw the position he and the girls were in, he smiled sheepishly. "I didn't do much good barging in that way, did I?" he said.

"You were wonderful," said Jane.

"It was some fight while it lasted!" Mae told him.

Johnny tested the ropes that tied him, but found no encouraging looseness. "No way to get free of them," he said. "At least no way that I know about."

"There must be," said Jane. "In all the books I've read the hero rescues the girl at the last minute."

"Guess I'm just a lousy hero," said Johnny apologetically, "or maybe they were lousy books. But don't give up hope. I have a feeling that we may get a break—if we can hold out long enough. Where's Frankenstein?"

"In there." Jane nodded to the other room. "Giving instructions about what to do to us."

"I've seen the ugly little monster somewhere before. Who is he?"

"Hirdy's chauffeur, Hans. He killed Angell and Ponds. He admitted it."

"So that's how it was done. And he's probably the one who's been pumping bullets at me, too. Sure—his car was downstairs last time. He's a bum shot. Hirdy ought to train him better."

"But Hirdy doesn't know!"

"Oh, no? Then how come his old man's name was on the list of the Fifth Column ring? He was one of Angell's contacts."

"You're just being vicious, Johnny Angel. You know very well Hirdy didn't approve of his father's actions."

"Well—time will tell. What else did you find out? Why was Angell's hand cut off, for instance?"

The girls shook their heads. "No, they didn't tell us that, but let's ask them when they come back."

"I think I know the answer," said Johnny, "but I'm not quite sure."

"What do you think it is?"

Johnny shook his head. "No—let's wait. We'll find out."

"You really think we have a chance? We might not be killed?"

"Don't give it a thought," he said airily.

Color began returning to the girls' cheeks. It is remarkable on how little hope can thrive. Jane said: "Johnny, just in case we don't—you know what I mean—if we don't see each other any more—I want you to know in spite of everything—I love you."

"Hey, hold on," said Johnny almost jovially. His job was to keep their spirits up and he intended to do just that. "What's all this 'if' business? What good'll it do me for you to love me 'if'? What I want to know is, will you love me tomorrow when we've settled this business with these rotten traitors?"

"Gosh," Mae broke in and almost smiled through her dread. "He really does expect to live through it."

"You can forget your expectations," said a harsh voice behind them. Hans had rubber-soled into the room. "Within a half hour you will repose quietly in a common grave out in the garden. Your two American friends are digging it now. It was most convenient of you to drop in, Mr. Angel. You would not wish the ladies to go on their long journey alone? No—I am sure you will be only too happy to accompany— What is that?"

Hans drew his gun and stood facing the entrance.

From outside had come the sounds of something between a steam engine and a calliope. The wheeze and clatter stopped in front of the door.

Mae thought fastest. "Be careful," she shouted. "He's got a gun!"

Hans brought his gun down sharply on the top of her curly red-head and she slumped into silence. He took a step backward, ready to administer the same medicine to Jane or Johnny if necessary.

The door opened and MacWilliams filled the frame, his own automatic ready. He took one hasty look into the room—then turned to Swazey, who was crowding him from behind. "O.K.," he said. "We got Angel. Now you go scouting around for my car. He must have left it somewhere close by. And when you find it, stick with it. I don't want it stolen again."

"But the girls—" protested Swazey.

"They're not here."

"But I'd swear I heard Mae's voice—"

"Refusing to obey orders? Go find my car!" MacWilliams barked—and gave Swazey a shove on his way before he could get a look into the room.

He came in and closed the door behind him quickly. Hans pocketed his gun and advanced to the detective. "Glad to see you, Mr. MacWilliams. We have captured the killer, as you can see."

"It's a lie!" screamed Jane. "*He's* the killer. He admitted it. And two gunmen are out in the garden digging our grave. He was going to kill us, too."

MacWilliams seemed not to hear her. "Thanks for getting Angel," he said. "And why do you have the girls tied up?"

"They would not cooperate," said Hans suavely. "Far from being willing to testify against this vicious murderer, they wished to shout to the world that he was innocent and that *I* had done the killing. Very uncooperative."

"Tch, tch," clicked MacWilliams. "Well—I guess I better leave them here and take Angel back. I want the credit for cleaning up this case!"

"I am sorry I must disagree with you, but you must see that it would be dangerous to take Angel back. He would talk. Suppose they came out here and found a grave? A grave is a difficult thing to conceal, you know. No, it will be much better if you leave Angel to me."

Mae was mercifully unconscious, but Johnny and Jane writhed under the effects of this conversation. Back and forth it went, Hans insisting that Johnny must disappear; MacWilliams demanding that he be allowed to take Johnny in.

A quiet, dignified voice interrupted them and all eyes turned to the door to see J. P. Hirdler, Jr., standing there. "You are acting like children," he told them. "The solution is very simple. Let MacWilliams take Angel with him—but with the guarantee that he cannot talk. Have you never heard of a prisoner being shot while trying to escape? The practice has been in vogue in your country for many years, Hans."

"Then you did know!" said Jane.

"I am sorry about you, Jane. I really found you most enchanting. I offered you a way out in marriage. When you refused, I knew that you must end like this. You knew too much and were intent on finding out more. On account of your curiosity, Ponds had to be eliminated. The man talked too much, and you were just the girl who would have been able to get him to talk and then fit the odd little pieces together."

"But you were shocked when we found him," gasped Jane, trying to make herself understand that Hirdy's consideration had all been an act.

"Yes. Hans is a bit of a butcher, don't you think?" He talked calmly and gently as he might have spoken to friends at a cocktail party. Hans stood grinning.

"So I was right," said Johnny. "You are really the head of a Nazi ring."

"You honor me, Angel. No, not I. My father. I am merely a lieutenant. And it is not a Nazi ring. It is purely American. Some of the most influential men in the country are in it. They have all dedicated themselves to the preservation of the American way of life."

"The Fascist way, you mean."

Hirdy shrugged. "Why quibble over words? We want the people who are best equipped for the job to run things. That's all. Nothing will be allowed to stand in our way. We are the ones who will keep America American."

"Yeah! By inviting Hitler in!"

"Heil Hitler," shouted Hans and jumped into a salute. No one paid any attention to him.

"Only Hans shares your mistaken view," said Hirdy coolly. "We do not need Hitler. We have plenty of men of vision right here in America."

"Phah!" Johnny spat. "Quislings!"

"I see there is no use continuing this conversation. Is everything ready, Hans?"

"It will be in a few minutes, sir."

"Now hold on a minute," said MacWilliams. "How are we going to handle this? I got Swazey outside. If he hears shooting he's liable to come running."

"You take Angel out before we settle with the girls," advised Hirdy. "If it comes to the worst you can silence Swazey, too. Yes, I rather like that. Why can't Angel kill Swazey in a gun fight and you kill Angel in retribution. You have some code, I believe, about handling cop killers."

"Swell!" said MacWilliams. "That's how we'll do it. In the car, after we get to New York. Nobody'll even know we were in New Jersey. And Swazey won't know what hit him because I'll be sitting behind him in the back seat with Angel. Swell idea! But I'll have to gag the prisoner first, so he can't warn Swazey."

Hirdy watched as MacWilliams and Hans working together forced a gag into Johnny's mouth and tied it tightly.

"Convenient for us, isn't it, Angel?" said Hirdy smoothly, "that some of our police officials think the way we do about Americanism?"

The two gunmen came in. "It's finished," said Whisper in a voice that was reminiscent of death.

"O.K. I'll take Angel now and get going." MacWilliams hoisted Johnny to his feet and pressed the muzzle of his gun into the small of his back. "Come on, you scum," he said. "Get moving."

If he thought Johnny would walk calmly to his death he miscalculated badly, for Johnny's feet were still free and could be used for other things besides walking. He lashed out and caught MacWilliams in the shins.

"That evens one score," he gloated to himself. In a moment there was a free-for-all going again. Jane used the opportunity to let out a few shrieks and Mae, who was reviving, joined her.

Hirdy jumped into action, pressing his hand over Jane's mouth and the Runt did the same with Mae. Both received bitten fingers for their trouble, but succeeded in shutting off the flow of sound.

With Johnny, MacWilliams resorted to his gun butt and for the second time Angel was violently helped into unconsciousness. MacWilliams hoisted his inert prisoner onto his back, Whisper helping him. "And that's that," grunted the lieutenant. "Now to find Swazey."

Whisper opened the door for him.

"You don't have far to look," said Swazey. He was in the doorway. In his hands he held a wicked looking riot gun—part of the official police equipment that had rested on the floor of MacWilliams' car. "I'm right here," said Swazey, "and I've been here quite awhile." He stepped into the room.

CHAPTER 15

"I told you to stay in the car!" roared MacWilliams.

"So you did, boss, so you did. And I told you I heard Mae's voice." He deftly abstracted MacWilliams' gun and put it into his own pocket. "Come on, now boys, get rid of your artillery, or I'll show you how a real gun works."

Whisper, standing exposed, obediently dropped a gun to the floor, but the Runt, thinking he had time for a shot, blazed away with his.

Swazey's weapon spat out a round of bullets and the Runt spun around and sank in his tracks. MacWilliams had dropped Angel and with young Hirdler, stood in a corner, white and perspiring.

It was almost too much for him to grasp—that the tables could be so completely turned by one man—and that one man, Swazey, whom he had held in such deep contempt.

Hans had used the diversion the Runt had caused to jump behind Jane's chair and kneeling there with her as a shield he drew his gun. "If you do not drop your gun at once," he called to Swazey, "I will kill you."

"Ho, ho," laughed Swazey. "A Nazi jokester!" At the same second he jumped behind Hirdler, using him as a shield.

Hirdy shouted. "Don't shoot—you fool. You'll hit me!"

"You think I care if I kill you?" Hans cried. "You were only using me, you thought. You would have killed me in the end when I was no longer useful to you. Well, I knew that. And I had the same plans for you. There is no American big enough to rule this country. That is a job for pure Aryans!"

"Heil Hitler!" cried Swazey.

"Heil Hitler," came the automatic response from Hans. His hand shot up. His head protruded above the chair top for a moment.

Swazey's gun went pop pop pop pop, fast and loud and Hans' gun clattered to the floor. Hans toppled after it, minus the top of his head.

Swazey released Hirdler, who stood, white and quivering. Then he ordered Whisper to untie the girls.

Jane's first act on being untied was to rush for some water with which to revive Johnny. When that young man opened his eyes he looked around in surprise. "Things have changed somewhat since I was here last," he said.

"Yeah," agreed Swazey. "The joint is working under new management."

"What happened?"

"Just a friendly little massacre! Here, you better hold this." He tossed MacWilliams' gun to Johnny.

MacWilliams took one last chance at a long bluff. "Look here, Swazey," he said. "You know you can't get away with this. My word will be taken against yours if you begin trying to tell any cock and bull stories."

"Yeah? What do you suggest, chief?"

"We'll take Angel in and let him stand trial. I'll give you a good report and see that you get a promotion."

"And the girls?"

"Why, we take them home safely, of course."

"Look, MacWilliams, I'm going to see you burn if it's the last thing I do. It's guys like you give the whole department a bad name. On account of your kind, I sometimes feel ashamed that I'm a cop. It's no soap, Mac, you're a dead pigeon."

"But you don't understand, Swazey."

"Stop it, Mac. You'll have me crying," said Swazey. "But say, there's one thing I want to find out. Why did they cut Angell's hand off? Like I said, I bet it's for some pretty ordinary reason." He nodded toward Johnny. "Johnny. You said you thought you knew."

"I think I do. Wait till I make sure." He advanced on Hirdler, who had completely lost his self-possessed Harvard manner and was allowing his teeth to chatter audibly. Johnny poked into Hirdy's pockets until he found a ring of keys. He examined them. One of them was very tiny. "Come on—out with the arm," he commanded.

Hirdler extended his left arm. A slave bracelet clung closely just above the wrist. It had a fancy little lock holding it together. Angel put the tiny key into the lock, turned it and flipped the bracelet off. He looked inside. "Just as I thought," he said, and showed the bracelet around. Inside was an engraving of a telephone dial.

"What in the world is that for?" asked Jane in mystification. The others were equally surprised.

"I'll explain it all when we get home," said Johnny. "Right now we seem to be having company. Better hold that gun ready, Swazey, until we're sure who it is."

There were sounds of many running feet outside, then a loud voice shouted: "Come out with your hands up. The house is surrounded."

"Oh, no!" cried Jane. "Not again!"

"Don't worry, darling," soothed Johnny. "It's not the gang. It's our friends—I hope. Best way to make sure is to use one of the prisoners as the target. Come on, Hirdy." He pulled Hirdy toward the door.

"When I open it, you step out," he said. "We'll find out quick enough who our visitors are." He pulled the door inward. Hirdy stepped out.

"Keep your hands up and walk this way," the voice outside commanded.

"Is Angel in there?" another voice demanded.

"That's Sam's voice!" Johnny shouted. "Sam! Bring them in, Sam. Everything's O.K. And hold Hirdler. He's one of the mob."

His words were drowned by a rat-a-tat of a machine gun outside. Hirdy had tried to run for it—but the bullets had caught up with him. His sprawled figure in the dirt road gave no indication of the many years of breeding it had enjoyed.

Sam Isherman rushed into the house, followed by a half dozen F.B.I. men.

"Welcome, Lafayette," said Johnny. "A little late—but welcome!"

They were crowded into Johnny's little living room. They had all slept, eaten, bathed, and the boys had shaved and looked none the worse for wear, except for a slight discoloration of Johnny's face—the only remnant of the kick he had received in his first chase of Whisper.

Jane sat next to Johnny and seemed to hang on his words reverently. Joe Foster was next to them, then came the big chair which carried the double burden of Mae comfortably snuggled in the seat and Swazey perched uncomfortably on its arm, his own arm coiled protectively around Mae's shoulder.

Their excuse for doubling up was the lack of chairs, but it could be plainly seen that both preferred it that way.

Gray-haired solemn Bill Lawrence sat next to them and Sam Isherman concluded the congregation. Copies of the morning papers were on the table, front pages showing pictures of the code deciphered, and blazing headlines telling of the roundup of the gang.

"I still don't understand, though," said Jane, "why Hirdy was wearing the bracelet."

"For the dial, darling. It's the key to the code."

"Yes, yes, I know that. You explained that hours ago. Even the papers know it. But why did he have to wear it. Aren't there enough phone dials around without wearing one? Or couldn't he have memorized it?"

"Sure—he did. This one happened to be Angell's. Angell was a contact man for the ring. Phone dials outside the city take many forms and maybe Angell couldn't memorize. So he carried his own with him."

"And," put in Swazey, "when Hans killed Angell he couldn't find the little gold key to take his bracelet off. He couldn't leave it for fear it would be a give-away—so he used his knife. See? A very ordinary reason, like I said."

"Yeah," said Mae caustically. "Ordinary. Like slicing a head off to remove a necklace. Wonder what you would do to get a tight girdle off, my hero?"

"Aw, don't call me that," said Swazey flushing.

"Well, you are. You were terrific!"

"All right. All right," said Joe Foster. "Keep that stuff private. What hasn't penetrated my skull yet is how did the G men get in on it?"

"I did that," said Sam. "When you called me and told me Johnny had lit out after the girls, I rushed back to the F.B.I. and told them about it. They had already digested the codes and were prepared for action. So we went."

"And now that MacWilliams has committed suicide," said Bill Lawrence, "Whisper is the only one left. I understand from the papers that he has agreed to turn canary and sing. Is that true?"

"Yes," said Sam who had been in contact with the police and the F.B.I. "But unfortunately he's not a key man. Just one of their gun mugs. Too bad we couldn't save Hirdy. He'd have been an important witness."

"How about his old man?"

"He denies everything, of course."

"But the codes specifically mentioned him and lots of others."

"Sure—but as they say—anybody could have written the messages. You know under our laws it isn't enough to know a man is guilty. You have to prove it."

Johnny's mouth dropped open. "Do you mean that in spite of everything these guys will be able to go right ahead with their fifth column stuff?"

"As far as the law is concerned, yes. But there are ways of stopping them," said Sam.

"For instance?"

"For instance, the H. A. plant was taken over by the government yesterday because of unsatisfactory production. Their first step was to put the Union Plan into effect!"

"Whoopee!" cried Johnny. "Now it'll be a real pleasure to get back to work producing those guns."

"And another for instance," Sam went on, "is Congress. The fat boys on the hill! The people don't seem to realize it yet, but those babies really jump when enough of their constituents yelp. Enough people yelled and *Social Justice* was stopped. If enough people got up on their hind legs and shouted they could get anything they wanted. The people are powerful and when they wake up to their power—"

"Never mind the politics," said Mae. "Just how does this ring thing work?"

"It's international," explained Sam. "They have groups in every country."

"How do they work?"

"Well, in every country the aim is the same. Make the Allies fear and distrust each other. Make the people within each country hate each other. Put white against black, gentile against Jew, boss against worker. Keep them busy hating each other. The old divide and conquer idea. Tell England America wants her Empire. Tell India and China they'll be double-crossed. Tell America it's playing the sucker. Make them all afraid of Russia and Communism. Then each nation, isolated from its Allies and fighting within itself, falls easy prey when its time comes."

Swazey shook his head. "I knew MacWilliams was a louse, but I never suspected—"

"Oh, he didn't know anything about the international complications. He was just one of their tools, captured by his own petty hatreds and prejudices. He really started to work on Angell's murder in earnest, when he was tipped off about the codes. Then he had to get Johnny instead of the murderer."

"Well," Bill Lawrence rose and stretched. "I'd better be getting on home. Work tomorrow."

"Me, too," said Foster.

Mae got up. "Come on, lieutenant," she said to Swazey. "Let's go downstairs. I have some private plans to talk over with you."

"Aw, gee, babe! Don't call me lieutenant. I haven't been promoted."

"Well, it says in all the papers you're going to get MacWilliams' job and a medal besides, hero." They went out after goodnights, still arguing the point.

When they had all left, Jane and Johnny looked at each other in silence. "Walk me home?" It was Jane who broke the silence. Her voice sounded funny—dry and brittle, as though it might crack.

Johnny said: "Sure—after a while. Let's sit here awhile. It's nice to be alone and peaceful again, isn't it?" His voice had the same tense quality as hers.

They looked at each other. Their eyes met and then separated guiltily. Johnny blurted out, at last. "Janie, darling, will you marry me?"

"I'd like to see anyone try to stop me!" retorted Janie.

Johnny leaped up, clicked his heels high in the air. "Oh, boy," he cried. "Oh, boy! oh, boy!"

Janie laughed lightheartedly. "I'm just as happy as you, darling, even if I can't jump as high."

Johnny grinned—a gamin's grin.

Jane became suspicious. "You're up to something," she accused. "You're leering like a fiend."

"I was just thinking—"

"Of what?"

"You will never know, now, whether butlers are born or made."

She laughed happily.

"Johnny, you won't believe how unimportant all that seems now. I feel awfully silly to think that the most important thing in the world to me was—"

"Don't say it," Johnny commanded, "until you see the wedding present I've bought you."

"This is exciting! A few minutes ago I didn't even know I was going to get married. Now there are presents already! Where it is, Johnny? Let me see!"

"Oh, no—it's not to be used until married."

"Oh, darling, don't be silly. Everybody says things like that, but nobody means it. It's like Christmas presents. Everyone peeks. Let me see, please, Johnny?"

"I'm just putty in your hands," Johnny grinned. "In here."

She followed him into the bedroom. He pulled a large, flat box out of the chest drawer and handed it to her.

"Nothing's too good for a woiking girl, I always say," Johnny announced solemnly.

Jane unwrapped the package with flying fingers, then stood as though transfixed, looking at its contents.

"Johnny!" she cried. "Oh, Johnny!"

The satin sheets glowed lustrously in their package.

COACHWHIP PUBLICATIONS
COACHWHIPBOOKS.COM

ANONYMOUS FOOTSTEPS | JOHN. M. O'CONNOR

COACHWHIP PUBLICATIONS
COACHWHIPBOOKS.COM

THE HEX MURDER

Alexander Williams

COACHWHIP PUBLICATIONS
COACHWHIPBOOKS.COM

THE
RUMBLE
MURDERS

Henry Ware Eliot, Jr.

COACHWHIP PUBLICATIONS
COACHWHIPBOOKS.COM

COACHWHIP PUBLICATIONS
COACHWHIPBOOKS.COM

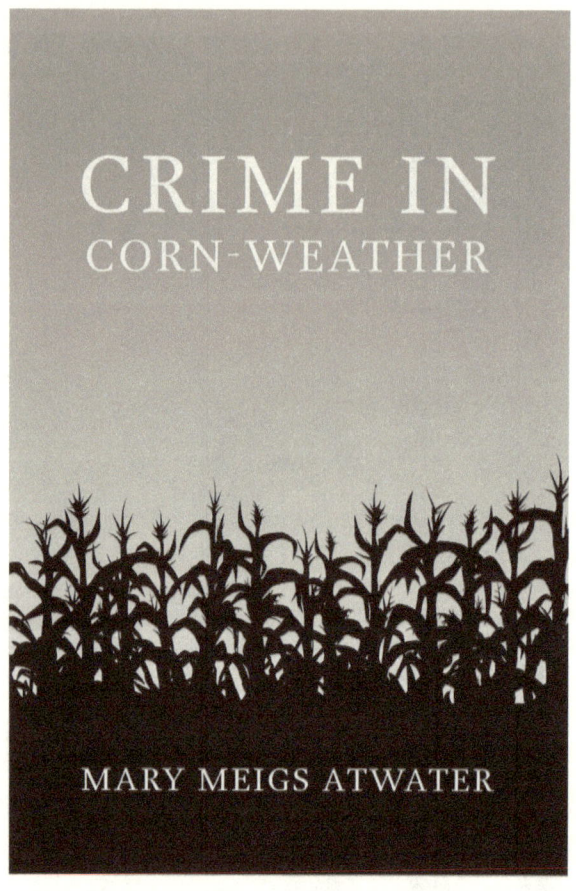

CRIME IN
CORN-WEATHER

MARY MEIGS ATWATER

COACHWHIP PUBLICATIONS
COACHWHIPBOOKS.COM

COACHWHIP PUBLICATIONS
COACHWHIPBOOKS.COM

MURDER
IN A WALLED TOWN
KATHERINE WOODS

COACHWHIP PUBLICATIONS
COACHWHIPBOOKS.COM

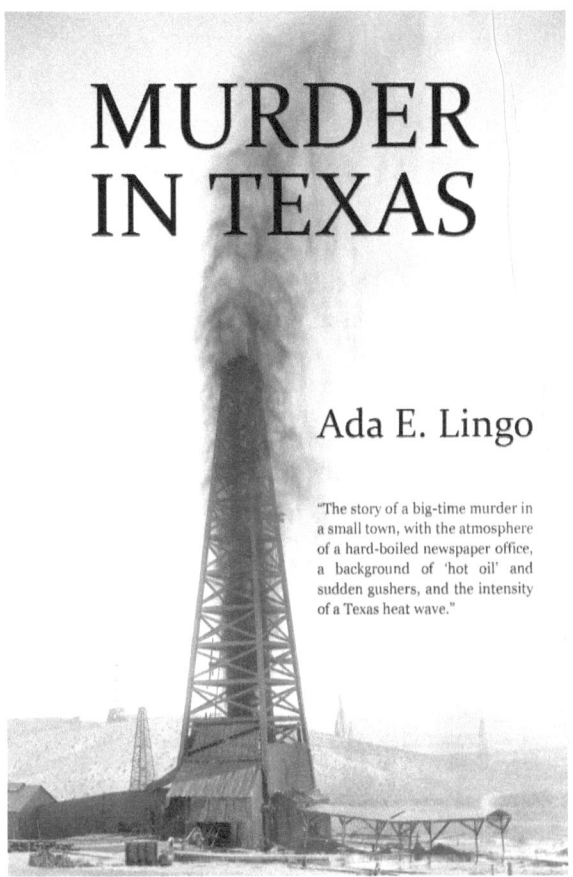

MURDER IN TEXAS

Ada E. Lingo

"The story of a big-time murder in a small town, with the atmosphere of a hard-boiled newspaper office, a background of 'hot oil' and sudden gushers, and the intensity of a Texas heat wave."

COACHWHIP PUBLICATIONS
COACHWHIPBOOKS.COM

THE LAST TRUMPET

A HUGH RENNERT MYSTERY

TODD DOWNING

COACHWHIP PUBLICATIONS
COACHWHIPBOOKS.COM

VULTURES
IN THE SKY
A HUGH RENNERT MYSTERY

TODD DOWNING